the late season

the late season

a short story collection by

STEPHEN HINES

TANGERINE PRESS • LONDON • 2017

Acknowledgements

Grateful acknowledgement is given to the editors of the publications where the
following stories first appeared: 'in early February' (*Pottersfield Portfolio*); 'the late
season' (*Gaspereau Review*); 'honeymoon' (*Regime*); 'in this field' (anthologised
in *Anthenaeum*, Bottle of Smoke Press, USA, 2010); 'what old 78s cost' & 'what
to do about the dog' (*this is affecting me exactly the way it should*, Pig Ear Press,
Malta, 2015); *this time, right here* (Sick Fly Publications, 2016). Special thanks are
due to Jeff Brouws for the use of his photograph; also Abbie Foxton for her much
valued input. The author would also like to thank Pete Lally and Michael Phillips for
their support and encouragement.

ISBN 978-1-910691-20-5 (paperback)
      978-1-910691-19-9 (hardback)

Table of Contents

the late season 11

a 1946 DeSoto S11 Custom Convertible on the first day of spring 22

the roads this time of year 42

honeymoon 47

in early February 55

in this field 63

what old 78s cost 73

what to do about the dog 81

this time, right here 90

we are careful 105

the book cellar 108

reasons why I can't sit in my favourite booth at Stillman's anymore 127

for Sam and Gillian

the late season

the late season

He pretended not to see her because she didn't want to be seen. He left her there on the periphery, barely seeing her movements. Her shoulder slanted into the wall, she would walk forward with all her weight leaning, letting the wall hold her up and then catch herself and back up, giving a soft rubbing noise. Like static, he thought. Her mouth hanging open in distraction, she stayed silent and stole looks at the window to see if her mother was watching.

He paced the edge of the pool, telegraphing his intentions to her, making large stage movements of picking up the pool net and cracking the thin layer of ice on the surface, stirring it. He put the net down and climbed up onto the diving board and stood there a moment. From that height he could see the trees just over the roof of the motel and he closed his eyes. There was a soft smell of fire somewhere and a small wind putting gooseflesh on his arms and legs and he opened his eyes and gave his belly a few loud slaps. He dove in, down to the bottom, the water warmer than the ice would have you believe. He broke the surface and gave three graceful strokes then stopped and rubbed water from his eyes. Small pieces of ice bumped him. He pretended not to see her eyes grow wider. He held his breath and sank to the bottom, sitting cross-legged. His heart in his ears. He opened his eyes and looked up at the underbelly of some leaves on the surface casting shadows around him. The soft patterns reminded him of his wife. Dancing with her. Those revolving lights they used to have in the nightclubs, with the coloured plastic filters. A clumsy box step and his hand at the small of her back, a spot his fingers had memorized as if there was braille there and for a second he thought of staying at the bottom. He tried to find a song in his head, one they had danced to, but all he could hear was the loud rushing sound of his pulse. His lungs burning, he pushed himself up and came out sputtering. He shook his head in memory of hair and pulled himself slowly from the pool and caught his breath. He rubbed his head like he was trying to push it in and looked around. He didn't have to pretend anymore because the girl was gone.

She had retreated, walked backwards into the office of the motel. Her eyes never left the surface of the pool until she was inside, and then still staring at the door as if she could see through it. Making sure the pool didn't leave her sight, allowing him to sneak up on her and catch her watching. She walked backwards past her mother at the computer, past the bell on the desk she wasn't allowed to ring anymore, past the complimentary coffee that had stood dry for days now and she didn't stop until she hit the far wall. She slid down and sat on the floor and waited for any strange movement or sound. She could feel herself floating in her body and wondered why she was, trying to put her finger on a memory somewhere but it slipped away from her and the feeling was gone. Out of her hands and through a crack and she stopped watching the door, her shoulders relaxing.

Her mother stopped typing but didn't look up, she just said Lily? What are you doing?

Lily didn't say anything. She got up and pulled open the back door and was gone. Running behind the motel, letting her hand trail behind her, her fingers landing on each doorknob of every room. When she reached the pop machine she punched every button and the coin return but nothing came out. She caught her breath and tried not to think of Mr Halliday and then she noticed the warmth of the sun on her back.

The light was different, coming down at an angle. A soft focus. Mr Halliday watched his breath go white in front of him. His car was the last one at the motel, had been for three weeks. Thanksgiving was gone, Halloween soon. Orange garbage bags of leaves with jack o' lantern faces lined the streets and Mr Halliday just stared at his station wagon. It might as well have had no engine as he gave no thought to getting in it and turning the key. Or he tried not to give thought to it, every time his mind stopped on it he pushed it away and he would go to the office and say Well, maybe just a couple more days. And he would leave quickly, avoiding their eyes, knowing what they would say when he was out of earshot. But he pretended not to notice any of that, just sat in his room and listened to the radio and took his swims. And all the time he knew he should leave them to their winter. Let them lock the door and walk up the hill to their house and settle into each other with no one else around. But he couldn't. The effort always stopped short, feeble and only half intended. He watched their patience stretch and waited for it to snap.

In the back of the station wagon there were carpet samples and linoleum samples and tile. Terracotta, limestone, faux granite, ceramic.

Samples of wood flooring. And books of price lists. Pages and pages of figures. A history of flooring in numbers. Not that he needed them; when each new price list came out every year he memorized them, spending hours in his office with a ruler covering the numbers and quizzing himself. His wife Margaret would hold the sheets and say Spanish Morning Red No. 6. How much per square metre? And he would close his eyes and say $17.50. If he was wrong she would pause to give him a chance to correct himself. He felt it was unprofessional to be scrambling through prices in front of a customer, looking unsure and incapable. To pass the time he would sometimes look at a room he was in and figure out how much it would cost to floor it. At parties when they became dull he figured how much it would cost to cover the floor in marble. In 1963 he figured that his brother-in-law's living room would cost $1800. In 1977, the next time he was back in the house, it would've been in the region of $6000, bringing him a commission of $480. And no deals for that fucker.

But now he could feel the numbers leaving him, coming out like sweat, almost happy to have them gone. His office would be calling, the phones ringing throughout his house. Kitchen, bedroom, office and rec room, ringing and ringing and no one answering. At first they would chalk it up to a few days off. Funny he didn't call in? To let us know? That's not like him. And the office would agree that it wasn't like him at all, but privately they were happy to have a few days off from him shouting figures across the room anytime someone had to look something up. But then they would begin to worry, calls to relatives would be made. No, haven't seen or heard from him lately. Soon there would be other calls saying Anything could have happened given the circumstances. Given the circumstances, he thought and pulled his robe tight around him. He eyed the sun and the window of the motel's office and took a flask from his pocket and tried to hide it in the bulk of his hand but the sun caught it and for a second he hoped no one saw it and then he didn't.

Mark, I think he's drunk. Mark?

Mark didn't say anything, just watched his hands on the coffee mug.

I think you should go talk to him Mark.

He looked up at her, her hands hipped, staring out the window at Mr Halliday. He paused and took a drink of coffee and didn't want to say anything but did. Liz why can't we leave him be? He could see her back stiffen and her shoulders hunch as if a string yanked them. He knew she was holding her tongue. Pulling a slow burn, she called it.

Mark. It's almost November. If we leave him be he'll be carving the Christmas turkey. She turned and looked at Mark but he was watching the coffee mug again. Mark. Come on. This is a bit excessive. Don't you think? I mean, Jesus, really. At first he says he's staying here for a few days and then every other morning it's a few more. Four weeks, it's been four weeks. We should've closed up almost three weeks ago. What's he doing here? Besides swimming and scaring the bejusus out of Lily.

Mark smiled when she said bejusus but she cut him off. I know I said bejusus. Just stop smirking and get out there and tell him it's time to go. She looked out the window again. Tell him he can stay for one or two days more but that's it.

Why can't you do it? he said.

She stared at him for almost a minute and he looked back at her until he figured there was no point in winning a staring contest and looked away. Liz made a noise through her nose and left. Making a point not to slam the door, but to close it so quietly it made no noise at all. He could feel her staring so hard through the door at him that it almost fell over. Then he heard her calling Lily's name and he sat and looked at the floor. Then her footsteps, walking away from the motel, the crunch of gravel in the parking lot. Small steps from Lily. Car doors and engine and gone. He stood up and went to the window and looked at Mr Halliday. He watched him take two quick drinks and look around. He spotted Mark in the window and they stared at one another until Mr Halliday raised a low wave. Mark thought he gave a nod in response but wasn't sure and Mr Halliday looked weakly away, sliding the flask down by his side. Mark could see him trying not to look at him in the window, his eyes slipping everywhere else, until finally he just closed them.

He watched him for a moment, trying to see Mr Halliday in a different context, trying to see him at a grocery store or at work or brushing his teeth and getting ready for bed and kissing his wife. But he couldn't. All he could see was the man in front of him, someone who didn't want to move or be moved, someone who didn't even want to be seen. Mark couldn't see him as anyone else but the person that seemed loose and untethered from the earth. He didn't know if he should try to help him or just let him go, letting him sit by the pool staring into space thinking about whatever was making him like this. Just turn his back until Mr Halliday was ready and then write up the bill and take his money and watch him leave. Maybe Liz was right. This wasn't their problem, their problem was that they were closed, the motel should be shut for the season, their life continuing without an extra person. I'm sorry Mr Halliday, it's like this, we're closing up, you have to go. We wish you well but you have to go. We'll offer you a 10% discount. Come back anytime. Please. But now you have to go.

Mark sat down in the chair behind the desk for a second to try and clear his mind but immediately sprang up and went out the door and headed for the pool. He looked at Mr Halliday and slowed down. Strolling, pretending to look like he was seeing if everything was running smoothly and looking surprised when he ran across Mr Halliday. And Mr Halliday seeing this, watching him with a small smile.

Mark. I know. I should be going.

Mark stopped suddenly, caught. He felt his body draining of something. He worked his mouth until the words came out. Mr Halliday, you can stay as long as you –

Mark. It's okay. I should've left long ago.

Mark was silent again, looking over the roof of the motel, watching the clouds. He tried to think of something to say but just shrugged. He shrugged again and said Won't Mrs Halliday be expecting you soon?

Mr Halliday gave a quick frozen smile and opened his mouth to say something but nothing came. He stopped smiling and lifted his flask and took a drink then held it out to Mark. Mark paused then shook his head.

Thanks. No. I don't drink.

Mr Halliday nodded and put the flask inside his robe and nodded again. They were silent for a time and Mark was about to leave when Mr Halliday said What would you do if Liz was no longer around? Or Lily?

He looked steady at Mr Halliday and said I don't know.

It's hard, I know. You don't even want to think of that possibility. But just try for a second. What would you do?

Mark folded his arms for a moment then unfolded them and put his hands in his pockets. Mr Halliday, I understand –

I'm sure you think you do Mark. But I'm not looking for understanding. Everybody is willing to reach out and touch your grief for a second and listen for a second. That's fine. That's nice. But I've had that. Now I just want to know what to do. I just don't know. Mark? What do I do? Tell me.

Mark shifted his feet and looked at the pool. Should he ask what is causing Mr Halliday's grief? Does he want to know that much about this person? He watched leaves bump against the sides of the pool, thought he should clean them out before they clog the filters, can leaves damage a filter beyond repair? How much do new filters cost? Should he get –

Mark?

Mr Halliday, I don't know what you should do. I don't have the first clue.

Mr Halliday shrugged and pulled the flask out and took a drink and said Well. Well neither do I. I just don't know. He looked at Mark and kept looking until Mark excused himself and went inside.

Lily sat in the car and tried not to stare at her mother. Her mother was driving too fast and once honked her horn at some kids that looked like they might walk out in front of the car and the shortest one raised his middle finger at her and Liz tried to place the kid, recognize him so she could call his parents later, but couldn't. She glared into the rear view mirror at the boy with his middle finger above his head and honked the horn again, a long note, thirty seconds or more, and Lily tried to ignore everything. She looked out the window and counted pumpkins and when she got to eleven the car stopped. They were at the Tastee Freeze and Liz got out and went to the PLACE ORDER HERE window and it slid open. A few minutes later she came back with two soft serves. They ate in the quiet and Lily had to stop for second because of an ice cream headache. Her mother didn't notice and Lily didn't say anything and when she finished her cone her mother sighed and said I don't know. I just don't know, Lily.

Lily looked at her mother and said Me either in a slow serious voice and Liz wrinkled her forehead at her. Lily stared evenly back and Liz started to laugh but Lily didn't join in.

When they got back to the motel Lily got out of the car and went into the office and looked out the window to see if he was there. He was, asleep by the pool. Lily went out and crept up to him. She stared a moment. Except for the hair he looked the same. But if he was dead how could he be here? Lily thought on this and her skin went gooseflesh. She tried not to scream and started walking backwards and when she thought she was far enough away she turned and started running, looking back once to make sure the ghost wasn't following.

That night they fought. Lily heard something break. Yelling and doors slamming and more yelling and then a slap. Then the night was quiet but no one slept. Lily listened for noises at her door.

In the morning no one spoke. They ate breakfast and when they were done Lily wanted to ask if they were going to church today, it being Sunday, but looking at her parent's faces she kept quiet.

They spent a lot of the time at the window, watching the pool.

Mr Halliday was cracking the ice. It was an anniversary of sorts. Forty years. Every day for forty years he had taken a swim. Regardless. Regardless of where he was or what day it was. Christmas day, his wedding day, even the day his wife died and the day after. The day of her funeral. That day, standing on the springboard at the Y, slapping his belly and hearing the hollow sound it made. Echoing through everything, somehow louder than the children laughing and splashing. Somehow louder than what was in his head. Into the water, the noise gone. Muted into nothing. The only sound, his heartbeat throughout his body. Pulsing behind his eyes, making everything vibrate, exaggerating everything.

He put the net down and got up onto the diving board and jumped in. He swam his lengths and got out of the pool into the chair not bothering to towel off. He tried not to think, but the whiskey he had had before coming out that morning was buzzing between his eyes, lubricating his mind.

He thought of the little girl, Lily, and how she avoided him, and the conversation he had with Liz a few nights back.

Why won't Lily talk to me?

Liz had been polite but distant, letting him know how she felt without words. She thinks you look like her grandfather, she had said.

Oh? And that's bad?

She's only seen pictures of him. He died a while ago, about six years before she was born.

Oh. I see.

I think she thinks you are him.

Mr Halliday had nodded but didn't say anything. He thought of himself there, haunting a little girl.

You do. Look like him.

I'm sorry, he had said.

He had meant for everything but Liz had just stared at him and finally nodded and left.

And now he knew he should leave. He could hear his wife's voice telling him to go, stop making a nuisance of yourself, scaring that little girl, shame on you. Get home, get back to work. People are worried.

Mr Halliday laughed and tried to push himself up from the chair but couldn't. He laughed again and vowed to stop drinking, hearing his wife ask him to please cut back to one or two a day for his circulation. He said her name, Margaret. He said it again, a little louder. He wanted to see the little girl again for some reason. Lily? She reminded him of Margaret for some reason. But everything now reminded him of Margaret, the water, the nervous quiet at 4 a.m., the noise the bed made when he turned over, the clouds. All shapes of her somehow. He smiled and sat back in his chair, hearing her voice. His vision blurred and he tried to get up again, not able to, his arms not wanting to push and he smiled once more and watched the sky and the clouds seemed to slow.

Later that afternoon Mark stood at the window. A wind was up but the sun was out. Leaves were coming down. He had been there for over a half hour. Soon Liz joined him and a half hour later nothing had moved and they watched him by the pool. The wind blew harder. Mr Halliday's mouth was opened. It took some time before they recognized his deep stillness and although neither wanted to go out there, one of them eventually did.

a 1946 DeSoto S11 Custom Convertible on the first day of spring

The service bell goes and he opens his eyes and looks out the window. Yawns and gets himself off the chair and out the door, the bell above it ringing and says Fucking bells everywhere and the driver says What did you say? and he says Fill up? No, two dollars. Nods, removes the cap, gets the nozzle. Leans against the car while pumping, trying to ignore the bits of dirty snow by the curb. Tilts his face to the sun and closes his eyes. Warmer than before but still not warm. Hey he hears then Hey louder. What? I said two dollars, stop the pump. He looks at the gauge, rolling past $2.25 and releases the lever. I'm not paying that extra 30 cents. Okay, he says. You're just getting the two, you hear me? I said okay, Jesus. The two dollars comes out the window and the driver pulls out shooting gravel and he sees the New Brunswick plates and says Figures and turns to see Walter looking at him.

What does that pump say?

$2.30.

How much money do you have in your hand?

$2.

Where's that 30 cents coming from then?

He shrugs and puts his hands in his pockets, shoving the money deep, trying to hide it.

From your pay, Jerry, it's coming from your pay.

Jerry shrugs again and looks back at the snow by the curb and then squints to the sky.

Are you hung over again?

Shrugs.

Jesus, quit arsing around. Quit wasting my money. Walter walks away and says I'm going in town, be back after lunch. Try not to fuck everything up.

Jerry watches him walk to his truck, feet splayed like a duck, and mutters Quack quack. Walter puts a pause in his step but doesn't stop and gets into the truck and leaves without looking at Jerry. Jerry goes to the snow by the curb and pushes it around with his shoe until it is thinned out. He looks up at the sun and back at the snow and watches it for awhile and sees a bit of melt, nods, goes back inside and gets his jacket and hat and pulls the chair outside under the window. Sits and leans back on two legs against the wall and puts his hands in his pockets and closes his eyes against the sun, wishes the fog of his headache away.

He thinks the bell goes but in his dream he's trying to reach a phone that's ringing but every time he almost has it in his hand it seems to move farther away. The bell again and he says in his dream I'm dreaming, wake up, that's the service bell, and he does and the chair smacks back down onto its four legs and he looks at the pump but there's no car. The bell goes and he stands up and sees Brian behind the pump jumping on the hose. The bell goes again and Jerry says Hey. Brian leaving the house with the screen door slap and his new sneakers on the porch squeaking on the morning wet. Down the stairs and slows and takes a wide arc around the front eyeing the door and windows to see for watchers, none there and puts his books under the front steps. Steps back to see if they can be noticed, doesn't think so but reaches under and pushes them back more just to be safe. Shoves the bag of lunch into his jacket pocket sure that the ham sandwich is crushed good now and in his head he can hear his mother say Doesn't matter, it's going to get crushed good with your teeth anyway, isn't it? What difference does it make? Looks once more at the stairs and says Okay to himself and turns and starts running without looking back and doesn't hear the screen door and doesn't hear his mother, only the gravel under his new sneakers and he puts on some speed and thinks he's faster in these than in the old pair. Runs fast until he's down the drive and onto the road clear of the house and stops to check the white sides of his soles and toe caps for scuffs. Nods and turns one corner of his mouth up when he sees none. Raises his head and looks up the road to town and down to the marshes and headed towards town, hands in the pockets of his jeans with his thumbs out and shoulders slumped and saunters. Like that guy from the movie he saw in town, always squinting and looking like he was going to ask a question but mostly stayed quiet. Moves to the middle of the road and wishes he had a cigarette, wishes he knew how to smoke. The guy in the movie again. Name? Can't remember, doesn't matter. Saunters some more until he hears a car and runs off the road and down into the gully and ducks until the car passes and decides not to take the road into town. Goes into the woods until he hits the river and follows it up.

After a while he wishes he hadn't, in the shelter of the woods there's still patches of snow and the ground that is clear is soft and wet and he can feel the damp seeping through the canvas and the sludge of his socks between his toes. Brand new and already soaked and will stink forever now. He thinks of a curse word and wants to say it out loud. Pauses for a second then says Shit. Smiles and shouts Shit and waits for an echo but there isn't one. Sighs and keeps walking until he gets to where the fallen tree across used to be until Peter Colville fell off and smacked his head and drowned and the Mounties had the tree cut up because Peter's mom caused such a fuss and who wouldn't? he thinks, your boy dying, no matter how much of a prick he was. Although he wasn't a prick to her, he was her boy and sons are never pricks in the eyes of their mothers unless they are truly awful pricks like murderers or rapists or something. Skipping school makes him a bit of a prick, but the forgivable kind and if he fell off a fallen tree and died no one would remember the little bit of a prick he was at times, just that he was a boy with a mother who loved him and wasn't that awful? One of the worst things ever? With a father long gone some-place else and his mother so busy now with her working two jobs, waitress and house cleaner, doesn't that make it all the more tragic? Brian nods at this and says Tragic out loud.

The late winter run off made the river swell and it's rushing pretty good now. A barkless branch the size of a baseball bat pushes along bouncing off rocks, catches against a big rock and pauses until the river is too much for it and flips it up and the sun catches it and it glints as if riddled with silverfish and for a second it looks like an arm rising from the water. Like Peter Colville back from the dead trying to pull himself out, reaching up to grab something, anything, Brian's leg maybe, to rid himself of the river or pull whatever he was grabbing at in with him. Brian stares at the branch trying to turn it from an arm back into the branch it is but can't and starts running, slipping on wet rocks, grabbing trees for balance. Runs until he sees the bridge just before town, slows and tries to catch his breath with his heart thumping in his ears like running footsteps. Stops and slowly turns expecting a decomposing Peter Colville to be lurching after him, but nothing. Smiles for a second then stops. Pulls his lunch from his jacket and unwraps the mangled sandwich and tries to eat it but can't, it's damp and gummy. Spits it out and throws the rest into the river and pulls the apple from the bag, staring at it until he just drops it to the ground, then the bag after it and gets up and climbs the embankment by the bridge. He thinks of mother making the lunch and him leaving it there and something drops in him making him wince and he slides back down the embankment and gets the apple, rubs it in his palms and climbs back up to the bridge. Leans against the railing and eats the apple, drops the core into the river and starts for town again, leaving footprints on the wood of the bridge. Looks down as he walks and sees dirty water oozing from his sneakers and mud on them and on the cuffs of his jeans. What his mother will say. He's off the bridge and onto the road past the bend and sees the gas station. Walter's truck isn't there. Brian breaks into a trot and his sneakers make a wet sucking noise and when he gets close he sees Jerry in the chair in front of the window. His eyes are closed and his mouth open, asleep probably. He creeps up, sees the rope thing that makes the bell noise when cars roll over it by the gas pump and steps on it. No bell. Steps on it with both feet. No. Gives a little hop with both feet and nothing them a big jump and the bell goes. Looks around the pump at Jerry, still asleep. Jumps again then again, keeps jumping. Hears a thump then a scuffle of feet and looks up to see Jerry watching him over the gas pump and Jerry says Hey.

Brian stops jumping and says How does this work?

Jerry points at the hose and moves his finger the length of it until it disappears into the garage bay. There's a bell at the end of the hose and air in it, in the hose, compressed or something. When the hose gets weight on it it forces the air to the bell and it rings. He stares into the garage. I'm not sure how the air makes the bell ring. Forces a dinger thing, maybe.

It doesn't go every time I step on it.

You're not heavy enough. You have to stomp on it hard. Or be a car. Jerry shakes his head fast. Anyhow, stop asking so many questions. You're doing me in. Jerry goes back to his chair and sits dizzy after getting up so fast and shaking his head. A bubble of nausea rising in his stomach and the head fog expanding. He closes his eyes and breathes deep and says I feel like shit.

Brian squints at him and tries to look hard. Were you drinking last night?

That sounded like another question. What did we say about asking questions? Anyhow, what do you know about drinking? What are you? Ten?

Brian frowns and looks away and says Thirteen next month. On the fifteenth.

Jerry looks him up and down and shakes his head, slowly this time. When are you going to start growing?

Brian looks at him then away and up to the trees to try and see some fuzz of spring growth there, the kind of blurry look you get when the buds start to open. He thinks he might see some but isn't sure, tries to remember what the trees looked like yesterday or the day before but can't remember. It's spring today, he says.

Jerry looks at the melting snow by the curb and says I know it.

Brian nods and says Aren't you going to ask why I'm not in school?

What?

Isn't that the first thing an adult asks when they see a kid out on a school day? Why aren't you in school?

What day is it?

Monday.

Jerry nods, says Right. Looks and doesn't see Walter's truck. What time is it?

I don't know.

Jerry nods again and goes inside, comes back out lighting a cigarette.

Brian says What time is it?

I don't know, I just asked you.

Didn't you go inside to check the time?

No, I went to get a smoke.

A smoke. Brian watches Jerry suck deep on it, squint, tilt his head and blow a jet of smoke from the side of his mouth like he was trying to get it out of him as soon as possible. Not like the guy from the movie. Can I try one?

No. It'll stunt your growth. Although by the looks of you, you been smoking three packs a day since you were five.

Shut up.

What?

Shut up. I'm not even the shortest kid in my class.

No? Second shortest?

Brian exhales loud and shoves his hands in his pockets and looks down and starts for the road then stops and turns after a few steps and says How's Beth doing? I hear she don't like you anymore.

Beth pulled her hair away from her face with one hand and gave the mirror a profile, frowned, changed sides and studied her eyebrow. Let her gaze move to her nose, the tip slightly indented, switched sides again, the indent less this side. Sucked her cheeks in and brought her free hand to her chin. Outlined her jaw down to her throat with her fingertips. Dropped her hand, let her face relax, released her hair back over her shoulders, sighed. Looked at Jerry on the small dirty chesterfield, staring into a can of beer in his hand, a fleet of empty ones on the floor surrounding his feet. She sighed again, louder. Jerry didn't look at her. She was about to sigh again, but stopped. She wasn't sure she wanted Jerry to look at her. Beth let her eyes wander Jerry's place. Not his, really, and not really a place. A room with a chesterfield and a hotplate and a fridge at the rear of the service station. Had to get the key from beside the cash register to go pee. No bathtub. Walter let Jerry use his every once in a while, in between he sponge bathed in the service station restroom. Get the key from the cash register, go outside and down around the back. Wash his armpits in the small sink, and, hopefully, his privates. Beth turned away, not wanting to think of it, unsure of what she should want but pretty certain this room that smelled like gasoline and sweat and beer wasn't it, wasn't a goal she could feel pride about achieving. She thought of Miss Langille, her Art teacher, who told her she should go to university in Montreal, Halifax at least. Would Miss Langille nod in approval at Beth here, now? She sighed again, not for Jerry's benefit, but because it just came out, she doesn't want Jerry to look at her, doesn't want anyone to look at her now, here, doesn't want to be here. But where can she go, things being what they are, and, really, what they would ever be?

You should get a rug, she said and immediately wondered if she really cared if he got a rug or not.

What? Jerry said.

He watched her as he took a drink from his beer. She saw his dirty fingernails, she thought she could smell him, a smell of unwash. What? he said again and she looked at his hands and let thoughts tumble in her head but she didn't let them reach her mouth and she said Nothing.

Jerry snorts and says What the fuck do you know about Beth? Or girls in general? You even have pubes yet? Any sprouts on that pimple you call a dick?

He looks at Brian and stops, he seems even smaller now, runs his eyes up and down the boy, lands on his sneakers. Brian sees Jerry looking at his feet and looks down, the gray and brown mush of his new sneakers sitting there. His ears go hot and he sees his mother smiling as she watches him put them on the first time and he hiccups but it isn't a hiccup and something rushes up his chest and everything gets hot and the not-hiccup gets worse and he tries not to sit on the pavement but does anyway and he knows the not-hiccup is him crying and Jerry says Fuck under his breath.

Jerry drops his cigarette, steps on it, puts his hands in his pockets and leans toward Brian. Stop crying, he says. I was just kidding.

Brian keeps the gulping sobs going for a minute and then starts breathing out hard through his mouth to try and stop then it slows enough for him to say I ruined my brand new sneakers.

Jerry stops himself from saying Yes you fucking did. He doesn't know what to say. It's alright, he says, but doesn't have any idea if it is alright. It's a pair of sneakers, are sneakers worth all this fuss? Were they special sneakers? he says and rolls his eyes at himself. What kind of question is that? How do you talk to people when they're like this? And kids? How the fuck do you talk to kids?

Beth said Nothing again and Jerry stared and he tipped his beer and tilted his head back until the can was almost vertical and she knew he was going to drop the empty at his feet and get another one. But when he got up he went to the door and opened it and took two steps outside. She could hear the splash of his piss on the pavement. Her voice surprised her by almost sounding like herself when she said The bathroom is twenty feet away.

Jerry belched and said Too fucking cold out.

She went to the fridge and opened it, counted seven cans of beer. She found the church key on top of the fridge, opened a can and took it to Jerry as he came in. He took it slowly and kept his eyes on her as he took a swallow and sat down. She went back to the fridge and he watched her as one by one she took the cans of beer and opened them and set them at his feet. When she was done she tossed him the key and it bounced off his chest onto his lap. She said I'm going to have a baby, and she left.

He looks at Brian on the pavement. The bubble of nausea floats in him again. It's okay, he says to Brian.

It's not okay.

No, Jerry says. Nothing is okay. Brian looks up at him with his eyebrows in a question and Jerry shakes his head and says Don't listen to me. Everything will be fine.

He found the church key in his lap and fingered it as he drank. He took the pointed end and pushed it into his thigh but stopped before it broke the fabric of his pants. He threw it against the wall and finished his can and reached for another one. He got up and went to the radio by the hot plate and turned it on. Waited for the DJ to stop talking. Too much talking, everyone just talks now. He finished the can and went for another one. Bent over and lost his balance and fell shoulder first into the chesterfield, bounced off and landed on the ground sending empty cans chittering across the concrete floor. Still talking. He leaned back against the chesterfield and sighed and belched and closed his eyes. Lifted a new can up and tried to drink without opening his eyes and the rim hit a front tooth, spilling beer down his chin and shirt and Jerry sent his tongue over his tooth, pressing it against the pain, sucking in his breath and stopping suddenly when he heard the song that was playing, had been playing, for a bit. He squinted and listened and paused and then started humming when the chorus began. He knew this one, it meant something to him, what does it mean to him? He hummed some more and remembered the song. "Downtown" by that Patricia Someone. No. A flower, or something like it, Beth loves this song, he made a special trip to Halifax to get the record for her birthday, Petula. Clark. Beth loves that song. It makes me happy and sad at the same time, she had said. Why? It's a pretty song and at the same time it makes me think of everything I'm missing. What are you missing? She had looked at him and he saw something fallen and hollowed in her eyes and he hadn't wanted an answer.

Come inside. Brian? Come inside. Jerry goes to Brian and holds his hand out and Brian grabs it without looking directly at it and Jerry pulls him up. Brian follows Jerry into the service station, the bell above the door seems too cheery to Brian and the not-hiccups almost start again but he pushes them down.

Sit down, Jerry said and Brian sits in a chair beside a table with a stack of *Field & Stream* magazines. He looks at the one on top, a drawing of a man in a river under tall trees on the cover. The trees seem almost too tall, they go out of the top of the magazine without end. Sun is coming through the branches in lines that shine on the man, a fly rod arched above him in mid cast.

Take your sneakers and socks off.

Brian pulls at his laces and works the wet things off his feet. Do you fish?

Jerry snorts. Not really. I just take a rod into the woods and sit by the river and drink beer for a while.

Oh. Brian looks at his white wrinkled feet. Mud under his toenails. He clears his throat and looks at the magazine again and looks at Jerry who is holding out a stack of paper napkins. Dry your feet, he says. Oh, Brian says and takes the napkins and begins working at his toes. Without looking up he says Did my father fish? Um, Jerry says and goes behind the cash register desk and down a hall. I don't really know, he says over his shoulder as he walks out of view.

Jerry comes back with a pair of work socks and heavy boots. He punts them in front of Brian. Put these on.

Quiet as the socks and boots go on. Brian feels a calming warmth from the too big things on his feet. Leans back in the chair and closes his eyes and sighs. You don't know if my father fished?

No. I didn't really know him. He kept to himself.

Oh. Brian tries to picture his father sitting by a river drinking beer but cannot focus on anything concrete. He looks at the magazine again and tries to see the man's face but it is in shadow and too small. It makes the trees in the drawing seem even bigger than before, so large that they shouldn't be able to stay upright on their own. Brian turns the magazine over.

Why did my dad leave?

How would I know that? Jerry takes the wet sneakers and socks and goes out a door to the service bay. Brian hears water running. Hears the sound of rubber soles being slapped on concrete. Turns in the chair as he hears a car pull in and the bell in the service bay dings. Watches Jerry go to the car and sees him nod at the window. Brian turns back around and closes his eyes. Inhales a smell of gasoline that is somehow comforting, feels sleepy. The bell above the door goes again but he doesn't open his eyes. Hears keys being punched on a cash register and another bell as the drawer slides open with a clatter of change.

Brian? He hears his name but it is far away and he hears it again and slowly breaks the surface of sleep. Jerry is standing if front of him with an opened can of fruit cocktail and a spoon. Eat this, he says. Be careful of the lid. I need a new can opener.

Brian eats the sweet squares of pale fruit, leaves the cherry for last. Spoons out the sticky syrup. Puts the can and spoon on the turned over magazine. Stares at Jerry. Jerry is watching him. What? he says.

Why did my father leave?

I don't know. I didn't really know him.

Brian looks at the clock. 11:14. Watches the second hand stutter around. Didn't Beth's dad know him pretty good? Didn't he ever say anything?

Jerry rolls his eyes and snorts. Mr Roberts and I aren't much for chit chats.

Jerry tried to stack the empty beer cans in a tall column but he couldn't get past six high. He kept losing focus and tipping them over. He tried doing it with one eye closed but it didn't help. He pushed himself up and to the door and stepped outside to piss. He watched the stream steam in the cold air and yawned and stared at the car parked a few feet away and lost track in his staring and started to put his pecker away and then realized he wasn't quite done yet. His underwear and fly got warm with piss and he pulled out again and finished. Tucked everything away and wiped his fingers on his pant legs. Looked down at the small bit of wet on his crotch and shrugged and almost stumbled over. He kept his momentum going and made it to the car. Opened the door and got in and took a deep inhale of the interior. Leather and conditioning oil. He reached his hand up and ran it along the rough fabric of the convertible top. Felt pockets for keys but didn't find any. Gripped the steering wheel and sighed and started to close his eyes and snapped them open when he thought of Beth. And letting her walk home. Pregnant? He shook his head. He always pulled out. Shook his head some more and a thought started in him that he didn't want to think and he leaned on the horn for a few seconds then quickly got out of the car and back into the station. He stumbled through to the front and picked up the phone and said Is she okay? when Beth's father answered the phone.

It's almost 2 a.m. Jerry.

What?

2 a.m. Why are you drunk and calling here at 2 a.m.?

Is she okay? Did she get home okay? The words sounded clearer in his head than they did when they left his mouth.

She's fine. She's asleep. She was upset when she got home, but we're getting used to her being upset when she comes home from seeing you.

Jerry concentrated on Mr Roberts' breathing, at least he thought it was his breathing, it might has been the noise on the line.

Things haven't been going well lately, have they Jerry?

Jerry slid to the floor, the cord caught under his armpit. I'm going to fix it, he said. Everything will be fixed, everyone will be happy and everything will be okay and she is never going home upset again and I shouldn't have let her walk home alone, and he wanted to say more but he has said all the words he can remember at that moment and just let his voice trail off.

Mr Roberts stayed quiet for a time and then said No in a soft voice and hung up. The click and buzz filling Jerry's ear until his chin dropped and the phone fell to the floor with a sharp heavy noise that didn't wake him up.

Brian nods and says I think my mother wanted him to leave. My Nan said he proposed and mom said no and he gave her some money that she took at first but gave it back to him except for ten dollars that she already spent on food, but said she would mail it to him when she got it but that he should just go.

I don't know anything about it.

You don't think he left because he didn't want to have me, do you? Do dads do that sometimes?

Jerry listens to Brian, his voice steady. I don't know Brian. I'm sure he wanted you. Your mom wanted what she wanted. It seems like he wasn't it. Things are hard between adults sometimes.

Brian looks at the boots at the end of his legs, like heavy weights holding him in place. That doesn't sound like an answer, he said.

Jerry slowly shakes his head and says No it doesn't. He thinks of Beth and doesn't want to think of Beth and says No it doesn't again and goes to the rear of the station and comes back jingling keys. Come on, he says to Brian and Brian gets up and follows him outside around to the back to the small parking lot. Jerry stops in front of the car. Puts his hands on his hips turns slowly to Brian and smiles.

What?

Smiles bigger. It's running.

What? Really? You've been working on it forever.

Almost three years. Parts are hard to come by.

Brian takes in the bulging shape of the car. It looks like the future and the past all at the same time. Paint a bit dull but the chrome sparking high in the sun. His eyes stop at the DeSoto insignia. He says the name out loud. It looks old, he says.

It's pretty old. It's a '46.

Brian figures for a bit and says That's like twenty years old.

Yup. Almost exactly.

Brian tries to give a whistle but it comes out dry.

Jerry whistles for him and jingles the keys again. Ride?

Brian looks at him. Aren't you working?

Yes. But I don't think I'm long for this job. Or this town for that matter.

Why?

Just a feeling. I need to sort things out. Make things okay. Get some money together.

How are you going to do all that by leaving work when you shouldn't be?

How old are you again?

Almost thirteen.

Old enough to be a smartass.

I don't know, Brian says.

I do. Help me put the top down.

Isn't it too cold?

We need the fresh air to help us think. Clear out the cobwebs. And it's Spring. Snow's almost all melted. We need to embrace and celebrate.

What? Are you still drunk?

No. Stop talking and help me with the top.

I don't know. I should get home. Bad enough I skipped school. Now going for rides. I don't know.

You're going to be in trouble anycase, right?

Yeah.

A lot?

Yes.

Your mom will be crazy mad about it?

Yeah. I never skipped before.

Let's see if we can figure a way she won't be so mad.

How?

Help me get the top down and let's take a ride and think on it.

I don't know. Brian looks over his shoulder and scans the road.

You say I don't know a lot. You shouldn't be skipping school.

Brian looks at Jerry and back to the road. Jerry takes out his cigarettes and lights one and taps Brian on the shoulder and Brian looks at the cigarette being motioned to him and pauses and sighs and takes the cigarette and puts it between his lips and squints and slouches and tries to make his silence say everything.

Jerry watches him and shakes his head and says Okay, come on. Put your hands here and here. He points to where Brian should hold the top. He goes around the other side of the car and puts his hands on the same spots. On three? Counts three and canvas and metal moves and folds and stows away and Jerry smiles and lights his own cigarette. He looks at Brian. He hasn't inhaled yet, just left the cigarette perched trembling on his lips. Squints for real now because the smoke is in his eyes and makes them water.

You can take it out of your mouth.

I know it, he says but doesn't.

Okay. Let's go, Jerry says and opens the door and gets in. He motions his head for Brian to get in the other side. Brian nods but doesn't move. Gets out of his slouch and touches the cigarette and puckers his lips in a big inhale. The space between the intake and the machine gun shot of cough is small but Brian keeps the cigarette desperately pinched between his lips like he is underwater and it is the hollow reed breaking the surface allowing him to breath and stay alive. He gets in the car still coughing and somehow says Let's go and Jerry starts the car in a rough rumble and they do, go.

The wind flurries ashes all over Brian but he keeps the cigarette in his mouth until Jerry reaches over and pulls it out and flicks it into the wind. Brian looks hurt for a moment, then relieved. He looks at Jerry and waits for Jerry to look back, but he doesn't. What are we doing? he says and Jerry says What? He repeats it, louder, and Jerry doesn't say anything and Brian gets a feeling in his stomach and says I just want to go home. Jerry slows down and pulls over to the side of the road. He gets out of the car and walks up the road for a bit then turns and comes back. Brian watches him, shivering. He sees Jerry smoke another cigarette while pacing. Brian's stomach moans and he thinks of his sandwich dropped in the woods. Sees his mother putting butter then mustard and a slice of cheese and ham on the bread. Tries not to see that anymore because it isn't making anything feel better, just making a hole inside him bigger and bigger. He wants his sneakers to not be ruined, he wants it to be yesterday, he wants his mother not to have sent his father away. Why would she do that? Why is she working two jobs and never home? Why is she making everything so hard?

Brian jumps when Jerry pulls the door open. It squeals on its hinges. Jerry starts the car and says I have an idea and Brian just nods his head. The car pulls out and goes for about five minutes and Jerry pulls into MacDonald's General Store. He looks at Brian and says I'm going to call your mom. Brian feels a rush of good go up his stomach and strike his head warm. I'm going to call your mom and tell her that I need some money so I took you and if she gives me money she can have you back as long as she doesn't call the police and I get to leave and you don't get in trouble. His voice trails off, his eyes working everywhere and they land on Brian who is crying softly with his head down and Jerry says Hey and Brian shakes his head and Jerry says I have to do something, I can't let things go on like this. It would be better for everyone if I wasn't here. He stops talking and sits for a moment shaking his head and Brian thinks he's changed his mind but Jerry squeals the door open and goes inside the store. How is leaving ever better? Brian says to himself. He watches Jerry through the store window. He is standing by the pay phone in back by the washrooms. He can see him looking at the phone but he doesn't pick it up. He stands there for a good few minutes then goes to the front counter. Shortly after he comes out with two opened Cokes and two foil bags of chips. In the car he passes a bottle and bag to Brian and they eat in silence. Brian burps softly from the bubbles and Jerry belches loudly but neither of them laughs. Jerry glances at Brian quickly and says There was no answer and Brian nods and says Okay.

At his house Brian wants to get out of the car so badly but doesn't. He looks at the door and windows and knows his mother isn't home. It will be okay, Jerry says and Brian shakes his head and pushes the heavy car door open and slowly gets out. Closes the door and awkwardly walks in the too big boots up his path and noisily up the wooden stairs. He hears the screen door slam and then bounce back with a softer slam and he can imagine the boy standing in the empty quiet as the echo of the slammed door fades.

Jerry reaches for the ignition then stops. Puts his hands in his lap, leans back and closes his eyes. Beth is there and he immediately opens his eyes and shakes his head and starts to breath quickly. He grips the steering wheel and hunches over it to try and calm himself. Breathes in his nose and out his mouth. Calm, he looks around. Sits up in the seat. Straight back. Go, he says.

the roads this time of year

What I should have said before you left, before I let you leave, into your car where you can't hear me anymore, what I should have said is please sit down for a second, what I want you to do is not rush, to take your time, and listen to what I'm telling you. Just take it easy, you know how the roads are this time of year, when it looks like it is clear, but it's not. Black ice. So be careful. Not that you won't be careful, I know you will, me telling you won't make you any more careful. Like those BABY ON BOARD signs in the back windows of cars, like they will stop people from accidentally hitting them. Not that I want to see children hurt in car accidents, just those signs seem redundant somehow and unhelpful and a bit annoying. But the roads, slippery this time of year, and always a chance of blowing snow especially in the Highlands. Keep sand in the trunk, bags of sand. It might help if you get stuck and also the added weight in the trunk helps for traction. And a shovel and a flare and a flashlight with fresh batteries and a blanket and matches and one of those protein bars. You never know. And be careful if you need help. Be careful who you get it from. I know you're a good judge of character but if you have a flaw it's that you are too trusting, too willing to see the good in people, if that's a flaw. But you're not that big of a girl, woman, you're not a girl anymore, I know. And you took that self-defense course, but you never know. Remember what happened to Ruby. Aunt Ruby, she said it was a good neighborhood and the man was well dressed and well spoken and the car was one like Dr McDonald drove, expensive but tasteful. And the man was so kind and said he'd drive her to the gas station. She was lucky to get away. If that ever happens to you, do what she did, keys to the face. Did they teach you that one? Something sharp to the face? To the eyes if you can. I know that sounds drastic and something you think you mightn't be able to do but I'm sure in a situation like that you could. Just do whatever you can because your mother and I worry. I know that's natural but we were so lucky to have you, after so many tries and the two miscarriages. I'm sorry to be talking like this but we worry, even when we shouldn't, we worry. And it's unfair of me to tell you all this, I know it's making you feel guilty and that's selfish of me, I know. I don't know what's making me think like this, but sometimes I get these feelings, like something is about to happen. Like that time I had the dream about the fire and the next day the neighbors' house burned down. Just a coincidence, I know, but it still makes me worry because what if it wasn't a coincidence even though I know it was?

But go, I'm being silly, just go and I know you'll be careful and you'll know what to do and I keep forgetting you have that cellphone now. Even though I don't like them they are good for certain situations, this being one of them. And I'm just being silly, me think-ing I'm psychic. I can't even predict the colour of my underwear. So go, I think too much, you'll be fine. You always were a careful driver, even when you were young and just got your license. She never told you, but when you first started driving your mother would follow you in her car, do you remember the blue hatchback she had? She would follow you to make sure everything was okay. Not to see where you were going or to make sure you were keeping out of trouble, just to make sure you were okay. She said you always used your signal and never speeded, or sped, whatever the word is, and never cut people off and always stopped for pedestrians. But it's not you we worry about, it's the other drivers, you can never know what they'll do. I'm sorry, that's enough, isn't it. You should go, before it gets too late, things are always worse after dark, that's what your Aunt Ruby always said. And even though she denied it, she was never the same after what happened. Always nervous and afraid to stay home alone and never drove again. And this is me just speculating, but I think it's the reason for Uncle Jon leaving her. I think she was afraid of men. Afraid of the possibilities of what men can do, no matter what their appearance may tell you. I'll stop, you shouldn't listen to me anymore. I'll just scare you and that's the last thing I want to do because fear isn't something you should think about, it stops too many people from doing things they should be doing. And if they don't do them young enough, well the fear just gets worse as you get older. Age feeds it somehow, everything seems faster than you are, simple things are threatening like two or more teenagers walking together towards you. Don't be afraid. I never wanted to be an appliance salesman, but I didn't know what else to do. The money was half-decent, at least when I started, and then I found I couldn't leave it. It's hard to step off into something you don't know. I didn't know what else to do. I was afraid of what was on the other side of the washing machine. I'm not making sense anymore. Alright, you should go. I don't know why I'm burdening you with all this and I don't know why I'm crying and you should go.

What I'm trying to say is that I don't want anything to happen to you that will make you afraid because I know what fear can do to people. You should've known your Aunt Ruby before what happened. She was something. One of those people that's always smiling and talking and laughing. Talking to anyone, people in bank lines, saying things like Isn't this lineup something? It gets worse and worse everyday. If we stand here any longer they'll have to call in a gardener to pull up our roots so we can leave. She talked that way. Even though she didn't care if she stood in lineups all day. She just talked that way, to anyone, just for the sake of talking and seeing other people smile. And that boy she went to her high school prom with, I forget his name, nice enough, but she could've gone with almost any boy, but this one she picked. It wasn't pity, she never thought she was better than anybody. She said the boy told her he wasn't going to the prom so she asked him. She said he'd regret it later in life if he missed his own prom so she asked him. And when Poppy died and Dad was in the war and couldn't get back Ruby stepped in and handled everything because Mom couldn't bear to. She was like that, it was never about her, it was always someone else, and that was taken away from her. That part of her that cared about other people was stolen from her. It's unfair, things are happening that shouldn't happen, it's not right, people get older and change, I know that, but it happens without us knowing. I'm sorry, stop listening to me, you should just leave, I don't know what's wrong with me, I've been getting like this lately, maybe it's the holiday season that does it to me, makes me sentimental and sloppy and drinking too much. I just get scared. I woke up the other night and I was walking down the stairs. I mean I was on the stairs when I woke up. Sleepwalking, I don't know. I've never done that before. I woke up on the stairs and my heart was pounding and I was hot and sweating and once I figured out where I was I just sat there on the stairs and closed my eyes so tightly they almost popped. I couldn't move I was so afraid. Don't be afraid, never be afraid. Never let anyone put fear into you. I'm getting old and scared and it's not fair and there's no one here that can make it stop. People aren't kind the way they used to be, people don't take the interest they used to. Remember, always be kind. I'm sorry, please. It's just. Don't go. Please. Stay. Ruby. Please don't go. You can stay, you don't have to go, I know you don't have to. Please stay. That's what I should have said, Please stay, before you left, I should've said Please stay and made you sit and listen to me for a minute, and say what I couldn't say, what I should've said but didn't, because men don't talk like that, do they?

honeymoon

Their wedding was quickly followed by a birth. Not the cause of the wedding, but close enough to have people talk. Water cooler talk, people making noise out of boredom but not really caring. In the spring her father died and the following spring his father. The fall brought the deaths of two uncles, his and hers. Hers not close to her, but to her mother; his very close, more like a brother than an uncle. The next spring his grandmother, old, a good life, but still. Then his brother, not like an uncle, but more brother than most brothers ever turn out to be. They tried to joke, hold the baby and joke. She said their seasons were marked by headstones but it wasn't the type of joke you laugh at.

The following year the fog of memory began to burn off and their laughter started to come more naturally, without the faraway sound it once had. Their daughter was four. Her laughter was always free but she sensed her parents' liberation and it became more frequent, open-mouthed and hands clapping in front of her. That summer they borrowed a co-worker's cottage on the bay. Two weeks they had, and after two or 3 days the neighbours made their way over, circling in shy fashion. Homemade wine and pies and common ground was found and the cottage folded itself warmly around them. Still nights spent on each others' patios and the children all making easy friendships, their noise in the close distance. The smoke from the bonfires still clinging to their hair and clothes the next morning. The ease of it all sifting through them.

One morning she took her daughter out on the bay, a small punt with an outboard. Back by lunch, she said and he took his coffee and book to the hammock. Three chapters and he fell asleep and when he woke up he was hungry and went into the cottage. 3:27. He called out their names but no answer. He went to the window and didn't see the boat on the shore. He checked the clock again. 3:29. He checked the one on the stove to be sure, a dead battery or a power outage or a blown fuse maybe, even though he knew the clock was changing time. It said 3:30. He stared at it until it went to 3:31. He started to run to their bedroom but made himself walk and picked up his watch and the numbers winked at him. He put it down and looked out the window and watched a squirrel hop to a tree and stop. It worked its jaws and looked out the corner of its eye at everything and then disappeared up the trunk. He tried to see the squirrel in the branches but couldn't. He heard it chatter and thought he saw a flash or tail but wasn't sure. He watched the tree for movement, wanting to see the squirrel again, putting his forehead on the glass and made himself breathe deeply, slowly. The squirrel didn't show itself. He went back to his watch and picked it up and stared at it. 3:46. Slowly he put it on.

Outside he looked up at the sun and tried to judge the time by its position but couldn't remember where east and west were. He closed his eyes and tried to picture the sunset, nothing. He went to the shoreline and watched the water, the small waves bringing nothing. He walked the length of the beach and passed a man walking his dog and they nodded at one another. He almost said something, but couldn't think of anything that sounded right. He walked back to the lawn and studied the cottage and tried to hear a cupboard door or the clink of glasses. He closed his eyes and waited but nothing came. He finally went to the nearest neighbour and talked to him. He put his hands on his hips to try and show his calm, his voice struggling for even. The neighbour listened and wrinkled his forehead a few times and finally said Hold on, and went inside. A few minutes later he came out and said I called a friend in the RCMP and nothing can be done officially yet, but he says unofficially he'll keep an eye out. Do you want me to take a run out? See if I see anything? He nodded and walked to the water again. The neighbour called his name a few times on the way to his boat but wasn't heard.

Word spread and throughout the rest of the afternoon people came. Small tinfoil packages of food cradled in their arms. They stood around like weeds, willing to feed his grief with a small, veiled eagerness. He moved away from them and kept his watch on the water. His eyes stopped at the small diving raft about fifty feet out. The night before they had swam out to it. Some wine in them and their daughter asleep. They lay dripping and watching the stars and he had tried to slip a strap off her shoulder, drunk fingers. She had pushed him away and dove in and swam to shore. He had rolled onto his stomach and after a few insulted minutes followed her in but she had already dried and climbed into bed and fallen asleep.

The noise of the neighbours brought him back and sent him closer to the shore. He looked at his watch and it was almost six and glanced at the sun and saw it leaning to one side of the sky and he knew which way was west and a flood of sunsets came at him so quickly he had to sit down. He saw them sitting with their wineglasses watching the bay open itself for the sun. The glow of dusk on his daughter and suddenly he felt like there was something inside him rushing from his feet to his head, back and forth, tearing his organs. He clenched his jaw to stop from screaming until it felt like his teeth would shatter. For a moment he thought of all the money he spent fixing his teeth, after years of avoiding dentists. Finally sitting in the chair and squirming although there was no pain, just the idea of pain, like monsters under the bed. Oh for fucks sake, his wife had said when he complained, try the gynecologist. Try giving birth. He had said Woman always say that. Oh fuck off, his wife had said. Fuck right off. But she had said it laughing. That's important, he thought, she liked to laugh and swear and drink and this is starting to sound like a eulogy and why am I thinking about the cost of my teeth? He tried breathing deeply and that calmed him slightly and in that small calm his mind started to wander again. There, he saw his wife and daughter and their capsized boat and they were slowly drifting apart and calling to one another, she telling the daughter everything would be okay, the little girl thrashing in the water and they drifted until the thrashing stopped. Or there, he saw his wife landing the boat on the opposite shore and taking his daughter and getting on a bus and driving far away and never contacting him and them starting life alone without him. And there, he saw his wife take their daughter from the boat and put her in the water and hold her head under and ignore the hands scratching at her, her face stone and cold and when there's no more scratching she takes the boat to the opposite shore and gets on that bus alone and leaving everything and he even thinks he sees her smiling on the bus.

He shook himself out of this and stood up quickly and began moving his arms quickly. He started walking in quick tight circles and kept shaking his arms as if the faster he moved the less he would think, but it didn't work. He saw himself coming here year after year, to this shore, staring at the bay and thinking Why me? or Why not me? or something like that, pity and grief. The first few years he comes alone and spends sleepless nights afterwards. Then eventually there is someone standing behind him, giving a respectful distance. They make a weekend of it, finding a quiet restaurant nearby and sleeping peacefully in a cozy B&B, his hand on her thigh and her nudging him when he snores. And then he stops coming altogether. Just small moments of thought given to it, maybe the way the new daughter's coughing reminds him of his first or the way the new wife squints in the sun just like she did.

Finally he let the screams come out and he pounded the heels of his hands into his head and then behind him heard laughter. He opened his eyes and turned to glare at the people, their laughter spreading and small squeals from some of the women and excited clapping. He watched them, unbelievingly, and it took him some time to see his wife and daughter standing there. His wife was talking; a laughing, excited story. She said Our engine quit, stopped dead, nothing. We had no oars. How stupid am I not to bring oars? Stupid. The current was taking us out the mouth of the bay, to the ocean. I started to panic, you know, like you would. So I jumped in and swam with the rope it my hand, pulled the boat behind me. Can you believe that? a woman my size? and swam to the closest shore and had no idea where I was. Just a dirt road, no one around, nothing, not even a raccoon, just tree upon tree upon tree. We just started walking. Hours. Then the man that runs the Quickway, Gordon, the one with the video store in it? he stops and gives us a lift. Everyone looked at the storeowner standing behind her and he gave a small smile and a wave. There was laughter and applause and his wife clapped as well and said You know what he said? He said we were going in the wrong direction. Typical. More laughter and clapping and their daughter skipped around the yard, letting the other children trail in her celebrity. His wife kept saying I'm sorry, I'm sorry, over and over and everyone laughed at her for her apologies. Soon the sun set and he watched it go down, staring hard as to never forget it. Patio lights came on and music from somewhere and he walked around in it and every so often someone would clap him on the back and shake his hand and the people started leaving. Left their tinfoil packages and wandered home, smiling at how something so bad could turn so quickly good. His wife told the story again and again, finding new details but emphasizing the same parts each telling. She paused occasionally to smile shyly over at him like they were at a junior high dance and eventually the last neighbour left.

In the quiet they linked their arms around each other's waist and their daughter pushed her way in between them. They took her inside and watched as she put band aids all over her feet and after each one she looked up at them and said Ahhhhh, making a show of it. Soon after they ate and she fell asleep in front of the tv and he scooped her up and bundled her close and went into her room. He stood above her bed, not wanting to put her down, just smelling her hair, tried to fix her in his mind like that. The sunset and this moment, never forget them. He stood there until his wife came in and touched his shoulder and he put her down and they both kissed her and went into the kitchen to open a bottle of wine. Stood at the counter, not talking much, just looking at each other and finished the bottle. He opened another bottle and they moved out into the warm evening.

He made a bonfire in the pit and a small sensation between his eyes started from the wine, a slight warmth in his forehead that slowly spread into his body and his thoughts started to float on the wine. His mind wandered through his daughter and he thought hard about the sunset and then he thought of the squirrel and then his wife and his mind lingered there and he remembered something and he looked at his wife until she smiled and said What? and he went inside for another bottle. He looked at the clock, it was something after 12, he closed one eye to focus, 12:23. He had a glass of wine in the kitchen before he went back out, banging through the screen door like he forgot it was there. From the fire she laughed at him, covered her mouth when the laughter turned to giggles and she couldn't stop. For a moment he laughed with her then stopped to listen to the fire, then the waves on the shore above it. Then he remembered again and couldn't stop and he started telling her what he had been thinking that afternoon, when she was gone and he didn't know if she would ever be back. He just wanted to match stories, to share her adventure somehow. He wanted her to tell him it was alright, to laugh at him and hold his hand and tell him that could never happen. But her eyes became flat as he talked, glossed over and when he finished she stood up and her glass fell to the ground and she left the fire until she became dark in the distance. He heard some noise by the shore and he stood up and finished his glass and went inside taking the bottle with him.

Inside he dropped his wineglass on the floor and cursed and then drank from the bottle. He wanted to go into his daughter's room but stopped himself and just stood in the middle of the kitchen drinking. He finished the wine and almost went outside to look for her but went into the living room and laid down on the sofa and tried to focus on the tv and the next thing the screen door woke him. He didn't remember sleeping. In the glow of the tv he saw his wife pass through the room. He didn't know what to say, he wanted to speak but didn't know how to start. Later, he blamed the wine and the fact that he just woke up and was confused. He used that as an excuse and people seemed to understand, understand enough so that it became his truth. His wife moved in front of the grey of the screen, slow and shadowed, not looking at him, hands rigid at her sides and he wanted to make a joke, joke like they did in times like these, but didn't of course, he let her go past but it was only part of her, she was mostly already gone.

in early February

She was a little under 400 pounds when she died. My mother, in her big bed, and when she went my grandmother said to open all the windows. Lord Jesus quickly. So her soul's free to roam and at peace. Then my uncle said The only thing that could fit that soul was the garage door, and my brother went at him and swung and my uncle's nose cracked and he didn't fight back. The whole time my grandmother is going through the house opening windows and my aunt screaming that she was going to join my mother in her grave because of the pneumonia she was going to catch if my grandmother didn't shut the fucking windows. Everybody stopped when she said *fucking*, my uncle holding his nose, and through the window I saw something, but it might've been the snow.

Geoff. Geoffrey. Come here. Geoff. My uncle was waving at me. The first night of the wake and he said Take this to your brother. A small piece of yellow paper.

I took it and stared at it and didn't want to go but he gave me a little nudge and I walked through everyone and someone called my name but I pretended I didn't hear and they didn't call again. He was in the kitchen mixing a drink and when it was mixed he poured some ginger ale into the shot glass and drank it down to make sure he didn't miss any of the whiskey. He saw me and said What? and his eyes looked lower on his face so I knew he had been drinking for a while.

Peter, Uncle Gerry told me to give you this.

He looked at the paper and bent down and held his hand out under mine and I let it fall and he pulled his hand away and it landed on the floor. When I went to pick it up he put his foot on it and said I hope he knows I'll break his goddam nose again, and I looked up at him and shrugged. He moved his foot and touched my head and picked the note up and poured me some ginger ale.

I thought he would throw it out and not even read it but he did and cleared his throat and went into the living room. I watched his back go until I thought I should go warn Uncle Gerry but I got there and saw them nodding and putting on their coats and walking to the door. They told my grandmother they would be back and left. Everyone went to the window and Mr McCarrol said they were taking it outside. We all got quiet and my brother and uncle went behind a snowbank and for sure we all thought a scrap was on but then a car started and we saw headlights pull away.

Oh sweet Jesus in Heaven, Mrs McCarrol said, don't let them kill each other in this snow. Everyone nodded and started talking and moving around and I wondered why it was so important that they didn't kill each other in the snow.

My mother had lost just over a hundred pounds before she died. She wasn't trying, she was sick and it just went away. My father had made plans for an extra large coffin but a normal one was okay and I think he was relieved but he never said and that night he just stared at it and I don't think it mattered what size it was. When Mrs

Connelly went to him and put her hand on his shoulder he moved away and looked around the room to see who saw and jumped up and said something like a bark and went upstairs. She saw me watching and came to me and sat on the sofa. She touched her hair and it was frizzy and grey. My grandmother's hair was smooth and soft and Mrs Connelly said Take care of him Geoffrey.

Pardon? I said. I didn't know what she meant.

She turned and looked at me and her eyes went right through me like they were looking at something behind me and could see it even though my head was in the way. She opened her mouth then closed it and opened it again a little wider and I could see her tongue moving around a bit but she didn't say anything. She got up and got her coat and left and everyone was watching and then looked at me and shook their heads but left me alone. That was okay by me.

I watched the coffin for a while but I couldn't really see her except for the hands crossed on her belly and the red tip of her nose. That didn't seem right somehow. Somewhere in the room was my grand-mother but I couldn't see her so I just shouted Nan and out of the crowd she came, more like a ghost than my mother was now. She sat down beside me quiet and I said Why is mom's nose red?

Hmm?

Why's mom's nose –

Makeup.

What?

Makeup.

Oh. Why?

Well. See. So she looks here.

She is here. Right there. I pointed at the coffin and my grand-mother looked at me and then the coffin and sighed and cleared her throat and then remembered the sandwich in her hand and lifted it to her mouth then stopped and let her hand slowly drop and cleared her throat again and looked at the ceiling and said Yes. Yes. I mean alive.

But she's not.

I could see her squeeze the sandwich. Bits of green bulged from between the bread. Yes, she said. Yesss. But that makes some people uncomfortable.

I watched her and she burped softly without covering her mouth and we didn't say anything more and she passed me the sandwich she was holding and got up and went into the people again. It was asparagus tip so I put it on the floor and got up and sat on a chair next to the coffin and she sure didn't look alive. Her nose was never red and it didn't smell like her so maybe it wasn't her.

Me small beside the coffin and people came by and said A pity about the weight, if only she lost some maybe this never would have happened. Someone else said I didn't know weight had anything to do with cancer. And the first one again said Yes. Well. Doesn't it? Healthy living and all? But I mean, God, really. I stopped listening then. Maybe I got so small my ears went away and I closed my eyes so they wouldn't see me and make a fuss when they saw I heard what they said and no noise and no light and I think I fell asleep, fell far away and for sure it was a dream when I saw my mother flying around the room banging into the windows like a moth and everyone is watching and she sees me and I run to a window but it won't budge and then the room is cold and someone is singing.

The singing was Peter and Uncle Gerry and the cold was the open door because they were back and I was awake and they were singing some song that must've made sense to them and Aunt Margaret was shushing them even though everyone was gone. They shushed her back and Aunt Margaret stopped and her back got extra straight.

Where have you been? She said it like an animal, like a growl.

We had to get supplies, Uncle Gerry said to the floor.

What? she said and Peter reached inside his coat and pulled out an empty bottle and set it on the floor and gave it smile like it just took its first steps.

And what are these supplies for? Aunt Margaret took two slow steps towards them, her back going from extra straight to hunched.

They looked at each other and Uncle Gerry seemed to have a plan and he was trying to use his eyes to tell it to Peter and Peter said For the Irish wake, and that must've been it because Uncle Gerry smiled and nodded and put his arm around Peter's shoulder and sat on the floor taking Peter with him.

The room quiet and Aunt Margaret's head moving slowly between them like an owl and finally she said Peter, love, we're not Irish, really, sweetie? Hmm? Then the room started moving fast and Aunt Margaret was hitting them with a bunch of flowers, I don't know where the flowers came from, and Peter was covering up but Uncle Gerry was just hiccupping into his lap and a flower landed in front of him. He picked it up and held it out to her and she smiled and stepped slowly in and reached for it but smacked him instead and his nose started to bleed. Oh Christ Jesus not again, he said and Aunt Margaret scooped me up even though I was too big to be scooped up and took me upstairs and I was in bed and the lights were off and no noise downstairs but in the next room I hear noises from my father that I never heard him make before. I hope you know the ones I mean because I don't want to have to tell you and I wondered why I wasn't making them and then I started too. Not because I thought I should but just because I did.

Then it was the day to put her in the ground. I was wearing my suit but it was too small for me now. My grandmother helped me get dressed and paused at the sight of me but said it didn't matter, that no one was going to be looking at me anyhow and she made me pull a sweater over the suit jacket and a coat on over that and then only the pants looked short and my socks were white.

The sky was the colour of pennies and the wind and all the ladies holding their hair. Some had scarves tied under their chins and they held on to those and we all stood in a circle around the coffin and hunched close together from the cold. I tried to listen to the priest but the wind took his words away so I looked around and there was no hole. At Poppy's funeral there was a hole in the ground but there was none here. I tried not to think about it and looked at all the faces and all the ladies were crying and I started too but the tears froze to my face and it hurt so I made myself stop.

Peter was beside me and my father was beside him. My father hadn't talked to Peter since the Irish wake thing and it was something that they were standing like this, I guess. It was like they were near each other but they were separated. A wall made from imaginary bricks or something.

Peter? Peter. I tugged at his arm but he ignored me. Peter?

He looked down at me and gave me a stare that was supposed to mean something and looked away.

Where's the hole? He didn't look at me. Hey where's the hole?

He gave me a small push and said Shut up.

I did for a second but then How come there's no hole?

Nothing then a sigh and he said The ground's too hard.

Too hard?

Jesus. It's frozen.

Frozen?

He was quiet and his face looked frozen too and he told me to shut up again. I looked at the coffin and back to Peter and said But where are they going to put her?

Shh.

But where?

SHHHHH.

But –

Somewhere cold.

Cold? It's cold now. The ground's cold.

I just told you the ground is too hard. They can't dig a hole until it thaws. Now shut up.

But where is she going?

He swooped and gripped my arm and pulled me up and said In the fucking root cellar for all I know. He dropped me and looked around but everyone was leaving so it must've been over and no one saw. A gust of wind and three hats came off some men and they wheeled away and the men chased them and someone laughed at the sight but the laughter was too heavy for the wind to blow away and Peter pushed me and left too.

They sent me back to school but that wasn't a good idea because no one would talk to me and one day during quiet time I fell asleep and must've dreamed because I woke up screaming and ran through the halls and when they caught me they said maybe it wasn't time yet and sent me home. Maybe it wasn't time yet for that either because no one talked to me there and we all walked around with our heads down and our eyes far away from everyone else's and our feet didn't seem to move when we walked. We just glided.

I took ways around the house to avoid the root cellar. I couldn't look at the door even. It was like that for a while until one night after supper I held my breath and went to the door and opened it and went down the stairs and couldn't remember where the light was. But it seemed empty and not all that cold and then a shadow in the door above me. We stood there looking at each other and I came up the stairs to him and Peter's eyes looked different. Soft somehow, and he moved aside to let me pass and I think he might've touched my shoulder, I'm pretty sure he touched my shoulder, and she wasn't down there.

in this field

Flannels and gumboots and the weight of water, the bay drew him down like smoke into its lungs. In the spring when he washes ashore the villagers semicircle him, watching and distant, no one willing to go close. With no doctor or undertaker in town, the priest calls on the truest Christian. People look away and stare at their feet. Nods and murmurs when someone says A priest ought to know a sin when he sees one.

Someone has to look after Gerald now, the priest says. Lord knows I would except for my faulty heart. Someone in the back laughs. The Lord knows who that was, the priest says. The Lord has an excellent memory. And He'll remember the ones that help Gerald now in his greatest hour of need.

He's dead now Father, he don't need nothing anymore.

Mae, you know better than that. Gerald needs to be put properly to rest. Now, hands for volunteers. Father waits and people start to walk away, shyly at first, mindful of the eyes watching them. And then with the dam broken open, striding with purpose, a pointed look at the priest.

Can't the Stabs look after him? Mae says. She takes a step closer, not going anywhere.

Who knows how long the Constabulary will take to get here, we can't have Gerald rotting on the shore.

At the mention of rotting, more people wander away. The wind almost stopping and leaving the smell hovering above them. Men and women with handkerchiefs to their faces, leaving with white flags of surrender clutched to their noses. Mae is the last, standing in the sunset, asking the priest questions. Where's Gerald's soul now? Purgatory? Limbo, like? Or straight to Hell because everyone knows he did it on purpose. Probably reached the bottom and held onto a rock to make sure he got the job done. Right?

The priest looks out at the water, the setting sun striking the tips of the waves and sending off sparks of light. No one knows he did it on purpose, Mae.

Well, God knows, don't He, Father?

Father looks at Mae and then Gerald and says You should go home Mae. Your father's probably getting hungry and the wind's got a nip.

He can feed himself and I ain't cold.

Just go Mae.

Mae shrugs and starts for her house, looking back at Gerald. Father looks at the village, salt grey and treeless. Buildings so few you could almost count them on your fingers. The General Store, Sarah Penney once said, is called that because it generally has nothing. The Noseworthys didn't like that, and it cost the Penney's store credit for a time until bygones. Rocks the colour of seals barely humping the terrain. Nothing to stop the wind when it decides to blow. And the rain when it comes is horizontal.

Father sits on a rock and knits his hands together and puts his forehead on them. It's some time before he hears a boat approach and then boots on the pier. The light of a lantern swinging.

Father? Is that you Father?

The priest looks up, craning his head up to the person above him. Dil?

Yuh, it's me Father. What're you doing down there?

Gerald came up today.

What? Confused for a second, Dil scrambles down to the beach, holding the lantern out before him and sees Gerald. Yes boy, that's his sweater. The loose checked flannels and gumboot. He lost a boot, Dil says and Father laughs. He don't look too bad for six months in the bay. Salt water, I guess, and the cold, hey Father?

I'm not sure, Dil.

I dunno, Father. Dil sits beside the priest. How come yer all sitting here?

No one would go near him to help me. Scared or something, like he's catching.

Oh. Jesus, he's ripe. Couldn't you even cover him?

The priest pauses and gives a small smile and says No one thought of it.

Sure. Poor Gerald. He probably didn't want nobody finding him at all. Probably wanted to stay gone.

We don't know that, Dil.

Maybe you don't, Father.

Quiet some more, both men watching the form on the beach. Then Dil says Hold tight, Father. He leaves the lantern and behind him the priest hears Dil grunt his way up onto the pier and the boots again back to his boat. He wishes Dil had taken the light, the flickering makes it look as if Gerald was winking at him. Soon Dil is back and throws to the beach a tarp, blanket, an oar and some rope. He hops down beside the priest and pulls a plug from a bottle, drinks and passes it and says Some medicine for your heart, Father. Drinks while Dil lays the canvas tarp flat next to Gerald. He takes the oar and works it under Gerald's lower half and rolls the body partly over. He ain't going to fall apart, is he Father? He repeats the same action for Gerald's upper half and works at him until he is square in the centre of the tarp. Wraps the tarp around Gerald. Hell of a Christmas gift, hey Father? Lays the blanket and with his hands rolls the canvassed Gerald into the middle of it and folds around and takes the rope and ties the ends off like sausage. He bends over and says Easy up, Gerald. Throws the body over his shoulder and does a little circle shuffle step until he sees the lantern, stoops at the knee to get it. Walks up over the rocks onto the road not saying a word, leaving the priest to watch the light of the lantern fade.

In the morning Dil's sitting on his boat lighting matches with his thumbnail and throwing them lit overboard. The flame gone before it hits the water. He remembers standing in the field behind the school-house trying to teach some of the boys how to do it. Lookit, he said, rattling the wooden matches in his palm like dice. Lookit. And he flips one up into the crook of his fingers, the head just over the first knuckle of his index finger. His thumbnail at the red tip and quickly pulling down and across and flame born but suddenly dead in the wind. Shit, Dil said and turned his back to the breeze and said Boys, get in close and lit another one. The boys whooping and clapping like it was Saturday night and shouting Hey Dil, show it again, and the racket bringing Dil's wife out of the schoolhouse saying I'd appreciate it if you would stop teaching my students to play with matches, Mr Skanes. Shielded giggles when she called Dil Mr Skanes until the look from her silenced and scattered them slowly home. And at their home her yelling and him not able to look at her, just her shadow on the wall from the light of the fire and saying I meant no harm. Harm? she said and started into something but he just watched her shadow move up and right down the wall, her voice growing dimmer until it was nothing and nothing left to her but shadow.

After sunup people start coming to the shore looking at the spot where Gerald was the night before. Dil hears Bill say The tide must've took him back out. Good riddance, Mae says and several nod. He sees the priest walking slowly towards them and Dil gets up and goes below deck to put coffee on. Ten minutes later he hears slow shoes on the pier.

Dil, you down there?

Come on down, Father.

The priest ducks below and settles on a chair.

Coffee?

Thank you.

Dil pours a cup and hands it over and then one for himself and sits down on the bed across from the priest and says How's the heart?

He smiles and taps his head and says That medicine you gave me was a mighty strong dose.

Got that on the mainland.

Well, you can't trust mainlanders, Father says. They both laugh. When he first came, all the talk was of the preacher with the city accent.

They sit and drink their coffee and Dil watches the priest hunker over his cup and says Cold?

A little.

Dil gets up and puts more coal into the stove, sits again and they finish their coffee in silence. The priest holds his empty cup in his hands and tries not to look at them shaking and puts the cup on the floor and tucks his hands into his armpits.

Dil picks the cup up and half fills it with coffee and half with what is in the bottle that he pulled from under the mattress. The priest looks away and pretends not to notice and accepts the cup. Dil does the same for himself and when he sits Father says Where'd you put Gerald?

Oh, in the basement of the church. Nice and cool there until we figure things out.

The priest nods and thinks of Sunday with the congregation sitting above Gerald and old Mrs Noseworthy whispering Do you smell anything off? He smiles to himself and takes a swallow and almost coughs it up because he forgot what was in there.

Don't waste any, Father.

They laugh and over that Dil hears what he thinks is the wind until he pays attention and recognizes *Pickles, Pickles*. Some kids had taken to calling Dil that and he wasn't sure why until Sarah Penney told him.

Pay no mind, Dil.

Dil shrugs and listens some more and tries to make the voices something else, something good like the waves or the fine fiddle that little Joshua plays or anything, but he can't. The worst noises can only stay bad. He gets up and goes on deck, ignoring the priest's Now, Dil. He stands and stares at the kids on shore and is surprised to see the beach also pebbled with adults. They all stand and watch each other and time stretches and stretches until the voices stop, petering out slowly. People start wandering away, not sure if they should be ashamed, looking at each other for clues. But Dil stays stock frozen until the last one of them is gone and then goes below deck and sits across from the priest. He says Did you tell them I took Gerald, Father? The priest says nothing and Dil stares until Father can't meet his gaze anymore. Dil keeps looking until he feels his look lose its meaning. He gets the bottle and pours heavy all around and catches the priest's eyes and says softly I wish you didn't tell them, Father.

Father makes a sign and nails it to the door of the church.

ATTENTION CITIZENS!!!
TOWN MEETING TONIGHT 6 PM!!!
ATTENDANCE REQUIRED!!!

Father stands outside the church at 10 of 6. No one shows until twenty past. Mae walks to him slowly and squints up and says No one is coming, Father. The priest watches her walk away up the hill into her house. When the door closes he goes inside the church.

Take us out, Dil, Father says and Dil loosens the lines and they motor out until the village is a dull smudge and Dil drops anchor. The wind is baby's breath. The evening large and clear and the water moving like the sheets on his wife's belly in the night. Dil looks away from the water onto the horizon. His wife has been gone for over a year. Left and shut the door behind her because she wanted to. A soft click of the lock and onto Todd Penney's boat and gone.

Don't let the bottle be a stranger, Dil, Father says and Dil puts some into the priest's cup. The village fades and cups get lower and Dil is watching Father stare into his drink until he says I'm sorry, Dil. Dil doesn't react and the priest repeats it, louder. Sorry for what, Father? Dil says and stares at him until the priest looks away. Dil's face flares red and looks at the deck and says No need for that, Father, it's not your fault. People go when they want to go. Whether it's across the water or under it. You can't stop them. The reasons are their reasons. Right or wrong has nothing to do with us.

Father nods and holds his cup out and watches the dark water.

Give strong drink unto him that is ready to perish, and wine unto those that be of heavy hearts. Let them drink, and forget his poverty, and remember his misery no more, Father says into his cup. Proverbs chapter 31, verse something or other, he says and laughs. Six or seven, I think. Or both. Six and seven. It's six and seven, I'm sure.

I dunno, Father.

It's alright, Dil.

What?

It's alright you don't know, Dil.

Oh.

It's okay, Dil. We forgive you.

Okay, Father.

Their sins are not your sins. You can't be blamed for them. Go in peace.

That's enough, Father.

Go in peace. Ready to perish, give strong drink. Where's the wine? Our hearts are heavy, Dil. *Wine unto those that be of heavy hearts.*

Father, I'm taking us in.

They don't deserve us, Dil.

Dil pauses at the wheel and says You don't mean that, Father.

What?

You don't mean what you're saying. That's not you talking, Father.

The priest shrugs and says I suppose not, and looks unconvinced at the water and then the sky and his head falls back and he doesn't shift for a time and Dil thinks he has fallen asleep. Dil goes to take the boat home and Father says without moving Keep an eye for the dove with the olive branch, Dil. It means there is land and all is forgiven and it is safe to take us home. Make no move until you see the dove, Dil. Promise me, you have to promise, Dil. Your soul relies on this, Dil. Trust me. Dil? Only you can get us home safely. Dil? Make it safe to take us home.

Dil says nothing and stands frozen until he hears even breathing and then heads them home.

There should be a box but there's not going to be one. Six feet? Dil jumps in and looks up at the edge above him and guesses close enough. Scrabbles out and rolls Gerald in and pays no mind to the awkward thud. Covered and crossed and named in crank grease with his finger, guesses at the dates. Dil walks to his boat and looks east for first light but no hint of it yet.

On his boat Dil watches the sun come up and when the heat of it reaches Father the priest stirs and slowly rises and leans over the side and lets it all go. Dil tries not to listen the best he can. Father eventually stops and struggles from the boat with barely a nod toward Dil.

Dil waits for someone to discover the grave in the small cemetery. Watches the town awaken and some boats leave for the day and laundry ghosts go up in backyards. He makes coffee and drinks three cups. It could be awhile before it's found. He thinks about going up and showing it to people. Just before noon he leaves the boat and goes up the dock and onto the path that leads to the bluff above the village.

No one speaks to him as he passes. Dil stands in the dry grass and imagines himself going to each person in the village and asking them what he did to turn them against him. Letting his wife leave him? Closing the door of his house and locking it and living on his boat? How can he fix it? Tell him and he'll ask for forgiveness. Apologize and look at his hands and humbly walk off. Will that fix it? Dil imagines doing this and knows that nothing of the sort will ever happen. He wouldn't apologize and if he did, no one would listen.

He takes from his pocket some matches and does his trick. Watches them burst and burn out and flutter in the wind to the ground. He does this one after the other until the grass starts to smoke. Turns his face into the wind until he feels the heat on his back and without looking goes down the path and out onto his boat. Sits and watches as the wind swirls the fire through the grass. Voices low then flaring to alarm. He sees the priest run from the church. Sees him standing and looking at the fire, his arms limp at his sides. Dil can almost see his mind turning, wondering which way to turn. To or away. Then Father runs to the person nearest to him, and then another. Minutes pass and a line of people forms from the shore to the fire. Buckets of water being passed hand to hand. And at the top of the bluff the priest with his arms stretched wide and his robes flying in the wind. Walking the line and leaning into certain ones to urge them on. Touching some on the back and clapping the efforts as the line speeds its progress.

Dil watches the smoke, dark and heavy in the sky. Starts his boat and casts off. Looks back once, not to see the village, but to make sure his wake is pushing him away.

what old 78s cost

He hears the clicking of the answering machine come on and sits up. The clock says 3:30. He sits straight up and reaches for the phone but just gets a dial tone. He gets up and tries to find his robe in the dark, not wanting to put on the light and wake his wife. She's the one who turns the ringers on the phones off at night. She sleeps with a sock over her eyes and earplugs. He can't find his robe and thinks it's in the bathroom and he decides to forget it. He leaves the bedroom and goes into the hall and checks the machine. There's no message. He walks into the kitchen and looks out the window and then to the living room and out that window but sees nothing. Watches the bushes, waits on moving shadows. Not even sure what he is looking for, as if the phonecall were a warning of sorts, but that doesn't make any sense. Just sleepy logic. He goes back to bed and lays there unable to sleep. There was no message, he thinks, go to sleep. It's fine, a wrong number, a drunk phoning an ex and getting the machine and the wrong voice and hanging up, or losing nerve before the voice and hanging up. Or ordering a pizza or a cab or something and getting the wrong voice and hanging up.

When the machine comes on again he thinks he's dreaming but

the clock is at 3:46 and he grabs the phone and says Hello? Watches the outline of his wife in the dark. This time there is someone and he listens for a while and keeps his eyes on the lump of sheets that his wife is under while he listens and says Okay and hangs up. He wants to wake his wife, but doesn't. Unsure of what to say and how to say it if he had to talk to her. He dresses and goes into the kitchen and writes a note.

Have gone to nursing home. Mom is gone. He scratches out *gone* and writes *missing.* He watches the cat come toward him and tries to think of what else to write. He gets the cat's collar and puts it on him. His wife takes it off at night because of the bell. He looks at his note and touches pen to paper hoping it might lead to the next line, something comforting and wise, but nothing comes. He watches the black circle of ink grow as it seeps into the paper. He hates these pens, he wants to write *I hate these pens. Why do you insist on buying these pens? They are ruining this note, this is an important note. A big black blob. My mother is missing and this pen is mocking me*, but he doesn't. He just puts S. at the bottom and leaves, letting the cat out with him.

There are two police cars outside the nursing home. Their lights are off and they sit silent and the moonlight makes them look like something else. Like something in a song from the '40s. Something that rhymes with moon and spoon and June. In the doorway of the home there is a small group. Two policemen with flashlights and three people in white. One of the policemen is laughing and one of the women in white says something and he stops laughing and turns his flashlight on then off and taps it against his thigh.

Mr Kelleher, one of the ladies says to him and steps out from the group and takes his elbow and guides him away to a corner by the door and lowers her voice and says Mr Kelleher, I'm Sandra. There's no sign of her yet. I'm ashamed to say we're not quite sure what happened exactly. She was there for supper, but she didn't show up for bingo. We checked her room and she wasn't there. We think she just wandered off.

He looks at the woods around the home and then to the policemen who are trying not to look at him and Sandra says We have a group out in the woods now. It's a warm night. I know it sounds strange to say not to worry but we have good people looking for your mother. She pauses and looks around. Your mother's a strong woman.

He wants to say But she's 83 and how exactly does a building full of professionals let an 83 year old woman just wander away and do you really think an 83 year old with diabetes and high blood pressure can spend a night outside in nothing but a bathrobe, if even that, no matter how warm it is? But he just nods and thinks how tired he is, how he just wants to go into the woods and stand there for a second and see her and say Hey, there she is, she's fine! and go home and slip into his house and take the collar off the cat and gently lift the covers of the bed and slide in without causing his wife to take the sock from her eyes, without disturbing anything. He takes a step towards the woods but Sandra takes him by the elbow again and leads him inside. He thinks of the robe his mother always wears, yellow flowers and light purple leaves. Mauve leaves and tiny burn holes in the right sleeve even though she doesn't smoke. People in white uniforms leading her by the elbow, looking at the burn holes in her sleeve but not realizing she doesn't smoke.

Liz, get Mr Kelleher some coffee. Would you like some coffee? she says to him, but before he can answer he has it in his hand. He's sitting in a large brightly lit reception area but the hallways shooting off are in darkness and there is a radio playing softly. Do you know this song? he says. He hums a bit of the song he was thinking of earlier. Sandra stares at him. It's a song I can't place, it's bugging me that I can't remember it.

Sandra nods and says I'll be right back. He looks at his watch and then at the doorway and the policeman is laughing again and he stands and begins to walk outside but stops and goes to the desk and picks up the phone. He tries to get an outside line, he presses buttons and lights flash but he can't get a dial tone and he bangs the receiver down and a piece of plastic flies off and Sandra is behind him giving a slow look and he says I'm sorry. He says it again. She pauses before answering, counting to herself. Done counting, she says Mr Kelleher, come sit down. Please. There's someone who wants to talk with you.

He sits and then a policeman and a man in a white coat are in front of him. It's a different policeman than the ones outside. They are both holding their hands in front of them, like in wedding pictures.

Mr Kelleher, the man in the white coat starts and he watches him talk for a while then the police officer talks and their mouths move and they shake their heads slowly and give apologetic shrugs but he hears nothing and just sits in the hard plastic chair shaped slightly like an eggcup.

Doctor, do you think it would be alright if I went home? He says and wonders if they have doctors in nursing homes and shouldn't he know whether they have doctors in his mother's nursing home. Isn't that something most sons would know about a nursing home where they put their mother?

The two men stop talking and try not to stare, try to work this one out in their heads. Wouldn't you like to see your mother when we find her? The officer says.

Would it be okay if I went home? He asks again and the three man stare at one another and the man in the white shrugs and says If you think that's best.

He nods and gets up and walks from the nursing home and when he gets in his car they start talking about him and someone says Shock and someone else says If it were my mother... and one of the officers says Well it's none of our business and I got enough on my mind and talks into the radio clipped to his shoulder.

In the car and the moon is gone, the road dark and straight and no lights on in the houses that tick by him. Maybe he knows he's driving and maybe he doesn't but the car straddles the yellow line. No other cars around but he straddles the yellow line and takes his foot off the gas and the houses beside him slow until they stop and he thinks he should be home by now. It seems he's been driving for days but time is the space between the brackets and there are no brackets. Is this what he's trying to say? Or maybe the brackets are too close together. Is that it? Or forget the brackets, no metaphor can say what he wants to say about time having no speed or limit, it just does. Leave it at that.

A car comes behind his and the headlights fill around him and he hears a horn and the car stops and he hears the horn again. Slowly, the car comes around him and the driver looks in and slows almost to a stop and Simon shakes his head at the driver who shrugs and speeds off. When the taillights are gone he pulls over to the side of the road and gets out. He sits on the hood and looks into the woods off to the side. He says Mom? Then says it louder and once more even louder and waits. Just wind in the trees. He stares into the woods and then closes his eyes and opens them quickly. Nothing, just wind in the trees.

He starts to hum something, then stops. He shouldn't be humming. Then he starts again so he can figure out what tune it is. He doesn't know. Something his mother likes? Maybe. He hums it again. No, he doesn't know. He keeps humming and it sounds so familiar. He's sure it's an old song, his mother would know.

I won't need these anymore, his mother said that day she was going into the home. I won't be needing any of this. Sell the furniture. It's not antiques but you might get something.

Mom, come on.

You might get something for the books. There's some first editions in there. Your father was always going on about first editions. Never made any sense to me, but talked like he knew what he was saying and wanted to convince everybody who would listen. Foolish. And the records, sell the records. There's some old 78s in there I know are worth something. They were my mother's. From before the war. She was a good dancer, but you never met her so it doesn't matter. Sell them, she said. She pointed to a small trunk on the floor. Those pictures, she said, those pictures, you can do what you like with them. I don't need them, it's not my life anymore.

Mom, you're being melodramatic.

She didn't answer. She just stared at him for a good minute and then went to his car to wait, taking the steps side on and one at a time.

And at the nursing home, they walked the halls that smelled like piss and rosewater, trailing behind a woman in a white uniform pointing out the dining room, the activities room, the exercise room, the reading room. Simon said This is nice, this is nice to everything and his mother said nothing, refusing to take his arm as they walked. Ignoring the elbow bent out in invitation.

Then later, after his mother's roommate died, she swore that Bob Barker was winking at her. He's a pervert, she said, and went back to her scrapbook. She had started keeping a scrapbook. One day when he was waiting for her to come back from bingo he looked inside. Clipped articles on physics and astronomy. One that ended *Instead, many experts now expect the universe to expand forever, accelerating faster and faster as eons pass, and to gradually dissipate like late-morning fog in San Francisco.* When he asked her about it, she was quiet for a while. Then said I don't want any priests or reverends or clergy types at my funeral.

What?

You heard me, she said and looked away. They were silent until she said Sometimes at night I wake up and see people standing around my bed. But then they fade away. She looked at him. Do you think they're ghosts?

No, Mother, I don't. Never called her Mother until she came in here. Separating her two lives for her. Before it was always Mom, now he separated her into past and present. No name for her future.

She said I don't think they're ghosts. Do you believe in ghosts?

No, I don't he said.

Right. Me neither. Then she opened her scrapbook, her fingers stiff and clumsy, like someone else was trying to move them for her.

His mother would know. She knew the names to everything. He stops humming and lies back on the hood and watches the sky and there're no stars and the moon is gone, wasn't there a moon earlier? No cars and no noise, just the wind and Simon gets up and into his car and he wants to go home and find that trunk of pictures and spread them all over the floor like constellations in the expanding universe and wake his wife and get her to stand with him in the middle of them all and look at them and put them into order. Chronological or family photos or holiday photos. Some order and just stand in the middle of them and point to each one and try to figure out who is who and why someone felt the need to take their picture and store it away for safekeeping. Arrange his mother's ghosts for her, guide them shifting and floating into a proper order. Stare at them until they become real and don't fade away when she tries to focus on them. But he doesn't. And won't. Simon turns the car around and heads back to the nursing home. He passes a gas station and almost stops at the payphone there to call his wife. But she wouldn't hear the phone and he doesn't want to listen to the phone ring and ring with no noise in their house and no one answering to talk to him and the machine picking up and hearing his own voice.

At the nursing home he gets out of the car and walks into the lobby and everyone is still there, watching him. He stops inside the door and everyone waits. He says This is affecting me exactly the way it should. No one answers. Maybe he's not making himself clear, not thinking clearly, but he doesn't know how else to say it. He tries to rearrange the words in his head to make more sense but can't. That's the only way it could be said. It's their fault for not understanding, not his. Please, you must understand, this is important, so much depends on this, you have no idea. Or you do, or you think you do, so please understand. There is noise behind him, some commotion, and he hears a short burst of siren but he doesn't turn around. Voices rising, the sound of feet running, but he leaves it behind him and just says all that there is left to say, nothing else could fix anything, with or without more time, he says This is affecting me exactly the way it should.

what to do about the dog

Something had to be done about the dog. I got to work late again the other day and now I don't work there anymore. Too many late arrivals, the boss said.

Okay, but what about the dog.

What?

How am I going to look after my dog, the food and his pills and those shots every once in a while?

What about yourself? the boss said.

I'll be alright, but the dog can't take care of himself.

Oh, well, I don't know, things will work out, he said. Tell you what, I'll buy you a drink.

What?

I'll buy you a drink.

Now?

Sure, why not? I could use one, he said.

It's not even 11.

When does that ever stop you?

It always stops me, I don't drink.

What? he said.

I don't drink.

What, really?

Yeah, really.

Well, shit, maybe this would be a good time to start, don't you think? On the occasion of you being fired?

I thought about that one. Counted my teeth with my tongue and thought about that one.

Well? he said.

I don't know.

Come on, he said, let me buy you your first drink.

Stopped counting my teeth. Well, I suppose I could.

Big smile and handclaps. That's the spirit, Jesus let's go, that's the spirit. Some of this spirit earlier and you still might have a job.

The boss stopped at a liquor store and came out with a bottle and held it opened between his knees as he drove. Here, try this, he said.

What is it?

Just try it.

Okay. Burned going down and a burp and burned in the nose.

That's the spirit, he said. That's rye, it's okay, it gets better.

We ended up at a strip club and he started ordering us drinks. Winked at me. Company credit card, he said.

From what I can tell, the girls that strip in the afternoon don't really care for their job. They looked bored and surly and one got pissed off and yelled something when not much money was thrown at her. Every once in a while the boss would look at me and say I'd fuck that. For one girl he said it 5 times. Tifany, with one F. Tifany, everybody. Give her a hand.

Are the girls at night any better? I asked him.

He stared at me a while and said What do you mean?

I figured out that you can hate your job and get in late and leave early and drink whenever you want and not know much about anything as long as you take your clothes off or are the boss.

I moved out of my place and lived in my car for a while and then sold the car. Then I sold everything else. It's amazing what people will buy. I sold my belt. I'm small and this guy was big. In a bar and he's holding up my belt giving it a right inspection and it looks like a wristband. I asked him what he wanted with a little belt like that and he said I got my reasons and looked like he mightn't buy it anymore so I shut up and didn't ask any more questions. The customer is always right.

And I quit smoking. No, I didn't. I just quit buying cigarettes. I smoked them when I could. It was summer and people left packs on their dashboards with their windows down and I smoked that way. I never took the whole pack, just one and moved on. I almost got caught. Lately I've taken to forgetting where I am and just stare into space. I know I'm doing it but I can't make myself stop once I start. That's how I almost got caught, standing there holding the guy's smokes in my hand like it was my dick. Threw them in the window and hauled it. Would have thrown my dick just as fast. The guy was huge.

I don't like asking people for things – money, smokes, pogey – but I found if I went into noisy bars I could make hand gestures and get the odd cigarette. If I didn't speak it seemed easier. Just make sure there's no cover charge. Most drunks are okay with giving out cigarettes, I find. Just so you know, 2 fingers tapped in a V against my lips means I need a smoke, so give over.

Then my diet and the dog's got very similar. I had a guy I knew who had an idea and wanted me to come along. I met him downtown and he had a sock in his hand that was toe heavy. Hey, I'm not mugging anyone, I said,

Me neither, he said.

Well, what's with the sock?

He swung it and it wrapped around his wrist and he flicked his wrist and it unwound. He yo-yoed it a bit and it was jingling. He opened the mouth of the sock and let me look inside. Loonies and twoonies.

How much? I said.

$65, he said.

$65 that made noise. What for? I said.

What?

I said what for?

I can't tell you.

Why?

I don't want to tell you.

Why not?

Because if I do you'll just try to talk me out of it.

Then why do you want me along?

He just stared at me until I said Okay.

We started walking. He said Do you have to take that dog everywhere? We kept walking and the street got darker and then the buildings weren't as high and we kept going until we left the city and came to an overpass.

He said Wait here.

I watched him go along the concrete wall and down into a gully that had some flickering light coming from it. A few minutes later I could hear him cursing and screaming. I was going to leave, but he came out. What was that about? I said.

Aw, I was supposed to meet a guy in the squat down there and I was going to buy a thing off him but it turns out there never was a thing so that is fucking that.

What were you going to buy?

He was quiet for a bit and was looking around and then he said A wheelchair.

I took a second to figure that one then said What for?

For panhandling. People are suckers for gimps. I know guys that lie down on railway tracks to get an arm or leg cut off. On purpose. Get drunk or stoned or whatever and lie down and wait for a train and then get social assistance and a fucking free ticket for panhandling, right? My luck, I lie down the wrong way, and then I got no need for money, right? You're lucky, you got the dog. Make a sign, NEED FOOD FOR DOG, that shit works wonders.

I didn't bother telling him I don't like doing that sort of thing. I'm a coward of sorts, you see. What's the use of having a philosophy if people don't know you have one? But nevermind, he gave me $20 for coming along so I don't hold anything against him.

That kept us going for a couple of weeks, me and the dog. Tinned everything. One meal a day for each of us. When it ran out I went to the unemployment office and filled out the papers and waited until I got to sit down with this woman.

Have you been looking for work?

I couldn't lie to her. She looked like a grandmother. Not mine, but a tv one. Soft and grey and smelling like rosewater.

Why not?

I didn't know.

I'm sure you'd have no problem finding a job. She waited. I was staring again. Sir? she said. Is everything okay? You're staring.

I know, I'm sorry, I said and left. I don't want any more jobs and I don't want to ask anybody for anything and I don't know why. I once read in a magazine about seasonal affectedness disorder which has something to do with not getting enough light affecting your moods but like I said, this is summer so it must be something else.

There's this joke my dad tells. A guy and his dog are in the desert and the guy goes days and days without food. Don't ask me about water, that isn't in the joke. Days and days without food and he's almost dead from starving and finally the guy has to eat the dog. He's done and licking his fingers and looking at the pile of dog bones and says Boy, wouldn't Rover enjoy those. But it's just a joke.

Something had to be done about the dog. One day I walked out to my father's place. It took 3 and a half hours. Years ago, when my mother finally left, she walked out and left all the doors and windows open. Left everything wide like she wanted the trees and plants and animals to come in and take over until the house collapsed under the ruin of it all. It didn't, but it's close. When I knocked on the door, my father tried to open the door against the clutter and stared at me for a while. He doesn't recognize people too well anymore. I had to take him up to my room and show him my old stuff before he said I know who my goddamn son is.

I asked but he didn't want to take care of the dog. I've had enough goddamn dogs die on me, he said. I can't take that anymore.

We had a drink. I'm getting pretty good at it, drinking. A few drinks. That felt good, better than the first time. Take the dog, I said.

He said What dog?

I showed him the dog.

I know what a goddamn dog is, he said. I can't take any more dogs dying on me.

I was drunk and said The dog's only 3, you don't have many years left in you. I was drunk, that's all I'll say in my defense.

He stared at me a time and his face got loose and I could see him thinking on that and he said Alright I'll take the goddamned dog. Can he hunt?

You don't hunt anymore.

I can hunt. He was screaming.

No, they took your guns away.

He stopped screaming and looked at the ceiling and said I can hunt, and went quiet.

After a bit I shifted to leave. Don't forget the dog's pills, I said.

I know what pills are. I know all about pills.

Tucked 3 pints of whiskey into my belt and left. He had whiskey bottles around the house like dust. Full and empty and getting to empty. Everywhere. I got down the road a bit when he came running after me.

Thief, you took my goddamn whiskey.

How could he tell? No, we drank it, I said.

No, there's some gone, jesuschrist, and you took it.

No, we just drank a lot.

He stopped and looked around like he was watching the trees for birds and then looked back at me and then the trees again. His eyes back and forth and after a time he said I suppose we did. I can hunt, he said, as if to make up for the whiskey mistake.

No, I didn't feel good about that, so don't bother saying anything about it. I was drunk. Maybe I'll see a doctor. The staring is just a symptom I bet. The magazine said something about shining a light behind your knees. I don't know.

I was going to sell the whiskey but didn't. One night I went out of my head with it, sitting in the woods taking turns drinking from each of the bottles. Pissing on my shoes then in my pants and vomiting on every inch of me. Next day I got up about suppertime. Out from under the bush I passed out under. Hunched and trying not to heave. Dizzy from something. My heart pounding everywhere, a thick rhythm echoing in the trees. Washed myself and clothes in the park bathroom and hung them from the branches to dry. People didn't seem to notice. A man in his underwear in the woods. Didn't even bother to tell their kids not to stare when they plainly were. So I guess not everyone didn't notice me, I stand corrected on that, a few kids did.

Next day I got a job washing dishes. No light behind the knees, just felt different. Work is what men do. The magazine didn't mention that, maybe they thought you should already know. A couple weeks pay then I got a room. The landlady smiled like I reminded her of someone. I didn't ask who, I don't like to pry and truth is I didn't want to know. Some people start talking and can't figure out how to stop. She seemed like one of those. On my feet, whatever I had went away, work is what men do. Maybe drinking does that to you. Or puking. I don't know. New shoes, haircut, shave. Wink at the waitresses, joke with the busboys about big tits and hockey.

It was time to get the dog back. I took the bus this time. The house is dark. Dark as it can be at noon. Knock and knock and knock until the door opens. He looks at me and then past me and back again and says I know who you are. I tell him about the job and winking at the waitresses. He doesn't say anything. I show him my shoes and he looks away. Maybe I shouldn't brag. I can buy you a pair, I say. He doesn't want any of that. I've had enough. I'm here to take the dog, I say.

What dog?

What do you mean What dog? My dog.

I can hunt.

What?

He ran off, he said.

What?

I don't know anything about a dog, he says.

this time, right here

There're questions. Times such as these, there are always questions. Worse, people asking them. Hunched in concern, hands held out gently like they are trying to corral bubbles, speaking soft. Are you okay? I'm fine. What day of the week is it? Thursday. Date? The fifteenth. What's your name? Simon. What. Simon. No, Simon what? Oh sorry, Kelleher. How many fingers? Three. Can you feel your extremities? Yes. All your fingers and toes? That's the same question. Any pain in your back or neck? No. Where do you live? Halifax. Street address? Leave me alone. You shouldn't stand up, please sit down. Leave me alone, please, I'm fine, please, leave me alone, things are fine.

It wasn't like they say, slow motion, it wasn't like that. It was almost a speed beyond speed, where things are skipped or missed, a filmstrip missing some notches and it stutters and hurries through the sprockets of the projector and then suddenly he is standing outside the car, everything broken open. His body humming with the noise of it, all the sound inside him, in the bloodstream, working through each organ. He wants to tell the people running toward him that they couldn't have possibly heard anything because everything had happened inside him, the film wasn't loaded properly is all. Just a technical issue, a temporary delay, and if they could be patient, things would be put right. He set his hand down on something, the car, the ends pushed in, an accordion, a squeezebox. *Mama works the squeezebox, Daddy never sleeps at night,* he sings and the people running pause, look at each other and nod. Then they do the hovering concern, gentle hand gestures, we talked about that already. Be grateful, he hears. Not someone talking to him, but from inside, part of the noise. Be grateful. He nods and tries, presses his hands against his head and closes his eyes and opens them again, looks at the car. Spiderwebbed glass and everything crumpled. Squeezebox, he thinks and laughs, that's not about an accordion but a woman's vagina. He tries again, tries to picture things, what his house looks like, where he works. He can't but those things don't seem important enough to remember. What his parents look like, what his wife looks like, his kids, his dog. Am I married, do I like children, do I have a dog? He doesn't know, he can't think of these things, can't picture them, doesn't want to. He thinks he might be dead, his memories taken from him at the gate, not allowed any further, this is the cost of being dead, sorry. He looks into the car to see if his body is there. No, but what does that matter? He could still be dead, couldn't he? He doesn't know the rules for being dead. Walks and touches things to make sure they are there, feeling for the permanence and tries to link himself to it. This is here and so am I, but he can't convince himself. Something plunges inside him and doesn't come back up and everything breaks open again and when the police come they have to chase him through the potato field beside the road and pin him against the earth and still him until the paramedics can catch up.

The police don't have much to ask and the hospital says he can go but please sign this, and here and here. Do you have someone to pick you up? No. Can we call someone to come and get you? I don't think so. Somewhere to stay? No, I'm not from here. There's a motel close, it's fine, The Blue Spot. Okay, that'd be fine, but I don't know where that is. We can have someone take you. Thank you, I'd appreciate that. The hospital has six rooms and two doctors and four nurses and one of the nurses gives Simon a lift but promises to take coffee back for the others. Simon says Thank you, and the nurse says No problem, it's nice to get out, would you like a coffee?

Simon looks at the motel sign and says Thanks again and starts to get out of the car. The nurse touches his arm and says Any sign of dizziness or pain or anything you call us, okay? Okay. The nurse gives a thumbs up and Simon closes the door and the car pulls away and toots the horn and Simon raises his thumb and looks at the sign again. The words are faded but the big circle in the middle of the sign is a fresh coat of royal blue. The sun is done and there is not much light left and the dot seems to float against the cracked white background and Simon stares at it, trying to stop the floating until a streetlight comes on and it slows the floating enough to make him look elsewhere, at the door, and he goes into the office.

Taps the bell on the desk, taps it again, just for the sound, not for the annoyance that the woman behind the desk thinks it is. Can I help you? Hello. Hi, can I help you? Simon nods and wants to tap the bell again and reaches his hand out to do so but stops and says Can I hit the bell again? No, can I help you? I can't hit the bell? No. Oh, okay, I'd like a room.

The room smells of bleach but the bed is soft and he stretches out with his hands above his head and eyes closed. The dark and quiet and empty space in his head is pulling him somewhere he doesn't want to go so he gets up and goes to the bathroom to splash water on his face. He watches himself in the mirror to see if his movements look familiar, like he has always moved. He can't tell. He smoothes his hair, unsure of how he usually smoothes it. He stops looking at himself, leaves the bathroom, leaves the motel room and goes back to the motel office.

The woman behind the counter puts her hand over the bell (*tngk*) and slowly slides it toward her and pulls it into her lap without taking her eyes off Simon. He says No, it's okay, I don't want the bell, I'm over the bell, I need something to eat and a drink, more than one drink, many drinks. Is there somewhere? She points over his shoulder and Simon looks behind, sees a small building across the road with a sign like the motel, only smaller. L'il Blue Spot Pub 'n Eatery. He nods, watches the smaller blue circle on the sign and says What's with all the blue dots?

The owner thinks they're lucky.

Snorts. Maybe for some.

You're not dead. You could be dead. That's lucky. She smiles without using her eyes. Simon looks at her, through her, and she says Aren't you the one from the accident? He starts singing The Who again in his head, doesn't know all the words, just sings the ones he knows over and over, staring at the woman behind the counter. She stares back, a minute or more. Returns the bell to the counter and taps it. Simon's eyes refocus and he says It's not about a musical instrument at all, it's about sex.

She tilts her head. They shouldn't have let you out. You're not right. She points to her head. Up here, not right.

Simon shrugs at her, sees her brown hair and her blue eyes, tries not to see her brown hair and blue eyes. Not sure why he shouldn't be seeing those things, glances down to her nametag. Marie. Marie, he says, I'm fine. Never felt better, just taking a time out here to catch my breath. Is that your real eye colour?

Marie sighs, takes her time nodding, looks down, looks at the computer, taps some keys, looks up again. Simon hasn't moved, he's smiling, using his eyes, his whole face. Marie shakes her head and looks down again. Try the Spicy Buffalo Chicken sandwich, she says and spins in her chair and pretends to reach for something in a low drawer.

Crossing the road, checking both ways, no traffic, he sees his car in the parking lot of a service station on a flatbed truck. The driver's side door is missing, doesn't remember it coming off or how it could. He stops and checks his pockets, finds his wallet and opens it. A thick layer of new twenty dollar bills. Puts it back and pats further for his phone. No phone. Should he be calling someone? He asked himself this already, didn't he? A wife? For sure he asked himself this already. Raises his left hand to his face, no ring. Feels the dark and quiet space opening in him again and shakes his head and says There's no need to be calling anyone, not right now, no matter who it might be, or why they are waiting for me, he starts walking again and inside stops as the door closes behind him and there is no one except the bartender and a man and a woman at a booth in the far back corner. The bartender nods and says Sit wherever you like and Simon nods back and sits at the bar and then gets up and takes a table nearest the door. The woman from the back booth gets up and gives Simon a menu. That's okay, I'll have the Spicy Buffalo Chicken sandwich. Marie sent me.

Sure. Drink?

Beer cheaper by the pitcher or glass?

Pitcher. Always by the pitcher.

Something dark?

Okay. Local?

Okay. Sounds good. And a shot of rye?

You got it. I'm Amy. She takes the menu and goes to the bar where the rye and pitcher of beer are already poured and she brings the tray back and Simon drinks the rye while Amy pours a glass of beer. She looks at the empty shot glass and back at Simon and raises her eyebrows and Simon nods and Amy nods back, puts his glass and pitcher down and goes to the bar where the second shot of rye is already poured and as she's carrying it back the man in the back booth says Amy, the pitcher is on me. Simon has the second shot and then a few swallows of beer and turns to the booth and says Thank you, I appreciate it, but, if you don't mind me asking, why?

You've had a rough day? The man gets up and walks toward Simon, his feet pointed out like a duck and he's not that tall but walks like he is and when he gets close points to a chair and Simon says Sure and the man reaches out for a handshake and they do and he says Albert and Simon says Simon and Albert sits and Simon says Pretty rough day, for sure.

Albert nods and stretches his arms above his head and brings his hands down into his hair and pushes it back from his face. Simon sees bits of gray, but there is more in Albert's beard than on his head and Albert, almost sensing Simon looking, pulls his hands down his cheeks and rubs his beard and sighs. He looks at the bartender and nods and

Simon hears ice and then Amy is beside them with a glass and puts it in front of Albert. Tall and clear, he swallows a third of it and sets in on the coaster in front of him and cleans a ring mark from the table by grabbing his sleeve up over his palm with three fingers and wiping in a circle. He looks at the wet on his sleeve, then at Simon. I own this place and the motel. He points out the door. And the service station. Some houses that I turned into flats that I rent out to the seasonal farm workers, apple pickers and such. He takes another few swallows.

You're a mogul.

Albert squints. A what?

Mogul. Have your hands in a lot of business ventures?

Oh. Mogul. Sure, that's me. Albert pulled the chain on a smile and then the fuse blew, brings his eyebrows in at the center of his forehead. How're you doing? With the accident? You okay?

All things considered, pretty good.

Albert nods, leans back and crosses his arms, uncrosses them and pulls a phone from an inside pocket, frowns at it, pokes at it, shakes it, frowns some more, says Fucking phone, and puts it face down on the table and glances over Simon's shoulder at Amy who has a basket and before she can set it down Albert takes it in one hand, replaces the phone with the other, grabs his glass and says I hate these fucking chairs, Amy remind me to buy new chairs. Simon, come sit at my booth. Nicer on the ass. Simon gathers his pitcher and glass and follows.

Albert sighs as he slides into his spot and puts Simon's meal on the table across from him. The Spicy Buffalo is good. Nice choice.

Marie said I should get it.

Albert nods and wiggles his eyebrows and sighs again. Raises his hands palms up in a *What can I do?* gesture.

She's pretty? Simon guesses. Doesn't guess that she's pretty, she is, just guesses that this is what Albert wants him to think because of all the histrionics.

Albert tries to whistle low but it comes out like a slow leak and rolls his eyes. Pretty? Fuck. Yes, but I've known her since she's been ten. Even her mother is younger than me. He does the palms up gesture again.

Simon says Mnh, a noncommittal noise he thinks, and takes a bite of the sandwich. Spicy, takes a breath and vapour from the sauce gets into his nostrils stinging and he coughs and water comes to his eyes and he puts the sandwich down and drinks what's left in the glass and pours another. Told you, Albert says.

Simon drinks half a glass and says You told me it was good, not that it would try to murder me. Wipes his eyes with his knuckle, gets the napkin and rubs his mouth. Looks at the sandwich, considers the ramifications, picks it up and slowly continues eating it. Albert reaches into Simon's basket and pulls at a fry, bites it, holds up the uneaten half and says Mind if I have a fry? Simon looks at him, eyes moving from Albert's chewing mouth to the half-fry held aloft, looking like a fast food Statue of Liberty and says *I lift my lamp beside the golden door.*

What?

It's written on the Statue of Liberty.

So?

So help yourself to the fries.

What do you care about it? You're not American are you? What do I care about the Statue of Liberty?

I'm guessing not much.

Right, not much. I'm not against it, but it has nothing to do with me. Simon nods. My ancestors came through Pier 21, Albert says while

Simon keeps nodding, which means I'm Canadian, which means I don't need a giant green lady to tell me to sing *Yankee Doodle Dandy* every ten seconds.

It was a gift to the U.S from France, Simon says but Albert has stopped listening, he's taken more fries and signaled for another drink and looks back to Simon and says Do you have a phone?

Simon napkins his mouth and looks at the smeared burnt orange on it and shrugs and says It might be in the car. I don't know.

Albert hunches in at Simon. You call home? Head shake. Why not? Another head shake. Simon can't tell him why he doesn't want to call someone, can't tell him why he doesn't want to remember if there is even someone to call because he doesn't know why himself. Doesn't know why he wants to stay here, trying to create a vacuum around himself that is of course impossible to create, too many things to compromise the seal and suck him into a black hole and spit him out into another space that he doesn't want to be in. Wait, is that how it works? Or is it a worm hole? He tries to remember his quantum physics, his Einstein and Feynman, his Hawking, tries to remember what he has read, shakes his head and remembers he's trying not to remember, wants to stay in this time, right here, and takes another drink, or tries to because the glass is empty, puts the last of the pitcher in and drinks it down. Looks at his basket, the sandwich is gone, the fries are gone although he doesn't remember having one. Albert says, Well, I need a phone and you need more drink, so… and he gets up and goes behind the bar for the phone and says something to the bartender and the door opens and in walks Marie.

She sits at the bar and a glass of white wine gets put in front of her and Simon begins to feel like he's looking the wrong way through a dirty telescope and knows he getting drunk, or is already drunk and decides to measure his drunkenness and rises to walk a straight line to the bar. Not bad, he says when he reaches it, reaches over in front of Marie as the bartender slides him another pitcher and whispers The Spicy Buffalo Chicken was delightful, and when he says the word *delightful* he knows where his drunk barometer reads. Marie takes a sip of her wine, Simon winks and smiles and nods, even though she isn't looking at him, and takes the beer back to the booth. Albert is already back, he says It's all set. Simon nods and says Good, although he's not sure what Albert set, but he smiles at the thought of something being accomplished.

The girls are skinny, too skinny, and from a distance look too young to be in a bar, but when they get closer Simon can tell it's just their clothes that are too young. Denim miniskirts and halter tube tops in fluorescent orange and green, respectively. A blonde and a redhead with side pony tails and red high heels. Simon watches Marie watching them wobble across the floor and timber into the booth, one on Simon's side, one on Albert's. Albert scans both of them and does a twirly thing with his finger and the girls look at each other and switch sides. Marie has turned back around but is shaking her head and Simon can feel himself shaking his head along with her.

Simon, this is Bekkie and Lexxi. They are twins. Well, not really twins, but I'm paying them enough so they can pretend to be and we have had enough to drink so we can go along with their pretending. Right girls? The one beside Albert giggles and covers her mouth and the one beside Simon, he decides to think her name is Bekkie, Bekkie tries to catch up with the giggling but it comes out too loud and sounds like a nervous horse. She looks horrified and Simon pats her knee and says It's okay, don't worry about it. Lexxi does the girl giggle again, sounding like a school uniform-wearing anime character, a perfect giggle, so perfect that Bekkie doesn't even try to match it, she just sticks her tongue in the corner of her mouth, tilts her head and twirls her ponytail between her fingers. Simon nods and says Stay with what works best for you, and she just stares at him.

Albert bangs his hands on the table, gives a *whoop* and pulls a wad of cash out of his pocket and calls Amy over. Amy slowly comes, shaking her head too, and Albert puts the money in her hand, holding on too long, pats it and smiles. Thank you, Amy, he says, the service was wonderful as always. Amy rolls her eyes, gets her hand back and goes to where she was standing beside Marie. Albert waves everyone out of the booth, and they all go, the girls leading, both taller than Albert, out the door into the warm night, although the girls have their arms crossed and their shoulders shivered forward like it was January instead of July. They pause and Albert takes the lead, across the road to the motel, goes to room 7 and unlocks the door and they all go in. There is a bar set up, new bottles on the desk in front of the mirror. Glasses and an ice bucket.

Albert puts his hand on Simon's shoulder. This was just going to be a *me* evening, but we can make it an *our* evening. He winks. Simon frowns, his dirty inverted telescope is now trying to look through a fog bank for land. Albert says Don't worry, no sword fights and opens his mouth wider than Simon has seen a mouth open and laughs longer than most jokes merit. Simon just frowns deeper, he has no idea what Albert means.

Something went missing, a block of time, because Simon looks at his hand and he has a drink that he doesn't think he got or was given and there's music and the girls are dancing just wearing panties and kissing. Simon looks but tries not to look. Albert is on the sofa wearing briefs and an open shirt, trying to nod along to the music but missing the beat every time in different spots. Simon quickly checks his own clothes, but he's fully dressed, nothing undone or mussed. He leans his head back and thinks of something. Why do you think they're lucky? The girls stop dancing and look at him, holding each other by the ass, palms cupped. Albert says What? Why do you think blue dots are lucky? Albert says Oh! like something jumped out at him and reaches to the floor for his pants and fishes his wallet out. Pulls out a piece of paper and unfolds it, looks like from a newspaper, creased and yellowing. He holds up a picture of a bright blue dot. When I was a kid, Albert says, the *National Enquirer* printed these with a caption of how you should cut them out and carry them around for luck or fortune or something. My mother was always reading that thing and always had a blue dot from it in her purse. When she died, I dug this one out. He smelled it. Still smells like leather and Rothman's cigarettes and Wrigley's. He stops and says shrugs. Or maybe I just think it still smells like that. He holds the scrap of paper out to Simon and says Here, take it. Simon shakes his head and Albert yells Just take the fucking thing. Simon puts his glass on the floor, pushes himself up, stumbles a bit, reaches for the paper, takes it and gets to the door, opens it and looks back. The girls are dancing again, Albert trying to nod to the rhythm, he's beckoning to Lexxi. The three don't notice him. He closes the door and stands in the quiet taking deep breaths in through his nose and out his mouth, trying to get to the other side of the fog bank. Holds the blue dot in front of him, lining it up with the hotel sign. They both swim, he thinks of Marie's eyes. He turns and looks into the window of the motel room. Only Bekkie is dancing now, Lexxi is on her knees in front of Albert, head in his lap. She pulls up, holding his penis which is slumped in her hand like a sunflower in mid–September. She sighs and looks towards the window, pinches some spit away from the corners of her mouth with her thumb and ring finger. She watches Simon, he thinks he sees her burp. She slowly shakes her head and Simon nods and turns back to cross the road and go into the bar.

Simon is sitting at the bar, a glass of water in front of him. He looks over at Marie and shows her the blue dot.

He give that to you?

Yup.

I thought he would never get rid of that. His mother gave it to him.

Simon shakes his head. He took it after she died. He thinks it smells like the inside of her purse.

Why would he give it to you?

Simon shrugs, he has stopped drinking but is still getting drunker. Maybe he thinks I need the luck, he says.

Marie snorts and turns to him. Her eyes got bluer since the last time Simon looked. I don't know about luck, she says, His mother killed herself after her husband, his father, left her for a younger woman. He hasn't heard from him since. His wife died about ten months ago, pancreatic cancer. Sick, diagnosed and dead within the span of two months. Albert's kind of come untethered.

Yeah?

Yeah, do you think ordering two hookers is standard operating procedure for him usually? For most normal people? He's been unhinged since Joanne died. Drunk all the time, hitting on every woman that comes close to him. He thinks he's some sort of business tycoon now, sold his pick up and bought a big fucking ugly Cadillac.

He asked me if I knew where to get cocaine. What do I know about cocaine? Marie shakes her head and picks up the fresh glass of wine that the bartender put in front of her. Jesus, she says softly before taking a drink. Some people can only take so much before they crack, I guess. Everyone cracks in their own peculiar way, I don't know, what do I know. I dropped out of university and came back here because I thought Halifax was too big. It scared me.

Halifax isn't that big.

She snorted again. I know. People laugh at me, think I'm kidding. Scared of a small city. Jesus.

Everyone cracks in their own way, he says. She snaps her head at him, eyes squinted, thinking he's making fun. She softens as she looks at his face that somehow doesn't look like a face at all, but something you see on a distant horizon in a movie that doesn't have a happy ending. She turns back to her drink. That's right, she says.

Simon finishes the water and puts the blue dot paper in his pocket. He leaves the bar and goes towards the service station, towards his car, stands by the driver's side and pauses. Climbs up onto the flatbed and leans into the car, brushing the diamoned windshield safety glass off the seat with his sleeve. Sits. Holds the steering wheel. Opens the glove box. Pulls out his phone and pushes at things, it's dead, throws it back. Opens the centre console, fingers some cds. Opens the thing that looks like an ashtray but isn't an ashtray. He touches some coins in there, touches something else, pulls it out. A gold ring, and what plunged in him immediately after the accident but didn't come up comes up now and he lets it, no more trying to stop the hole in his memory from getting filled, like he was trying to stop the dirt from going in a grave. He puts it on his left ring finger and thinks he sees something flash in the rearview mirror from the corner of his eye.

Looks but sees nothing. Yawns, suddenly so tired. Takes the ring off and puts it back in the ashtray that's not an ashtray. Sees Marie walking toward him. He sighs and rolls over the seat into the back, lays down. She says Are you okay? He says Can you take me home? She laughs, I'm not taking you to my house. No, please, he says, get in, not your home. Marie laughs again, says In this? but gets into the car anyway. Are we moving? Simon asks. Marie angles herself so she can she him in the mirror. Are we moving? he asks again. It feels like we're moving. Blue used to be my favourite colour, he says. She stays quiet, keeps watching him in the mirror. Watches him close his eyes, watches as his mouth relaxes and opens and his breathing gets deeper and even and turns to a drunk snore. She waits. We're moving, she says, Where do you live? She waits longer.

we are careful

We are scared living in the city. We do not go out. No, we do, but rarely. Late at night to the cash machine and back. Our clothes are ones that everyone can wear. Clothes so unnoticeable that they are almost not clothes at all, just a cloak to render us invisible. Soft sole shoes that make no noise. We are careful. We try not to open the door. We don't burn our lights brightly. Turning only a small light on in each room as we enter, and turning it off as we leave. Windows with blinds and curtains, never opened. We align our eyes to the cracks between the blinds and the window to see if the city is still there. It is. The television volume is now off. We started with it low, then tried the close captioning option but it took our attention away from the scrolling words at the bottom of the screen. BREAKING NEWS. So we trained ourselves to read their lips. The large, well dressed heads on the screen. We are good at reading lips now. So no more volume on the television. No music, never music. We cook food that doesn't smell too much, for fear the smells will escape into the halls and people could guess what we were eating and what that would tell them about us. When we need more food we order it on the phone. We give a name that matches our clothes. When the knock comes we slide a note in block print that tells them to leave the food. Then we slide the money out, with another note that says keep the change. We listen to them leave. We peer though the spy hole to make sure they are not trying to fool us. They have done that before. When we are sure they are gone one of us puts a glove on and opens the door enough to stick an arm out and grab the bag. If there is more than one bag, we close the door after we pull the first bag in and then open it again for the next. We repeat that for the rest of the bags. We are careful.

Someone comes to the door that we do not expect. No food was ordered. It is a loud knock, like it is angry at the door. We don't move. Stare at each other. We blink and the wet click our eyelids make seems louder than a door slammed. We are sure the noise of it will give us away. Another knock, a voice. We don't move. Or blink. We listen to them leave. We still don't move but eventually blink.

We can't sleep. No one wants to sleep. We barely eat, nothing is cooked. No television. No food is ordered. This goes on for days. We are tired and hungry, weak. We say this can't go on. We say we need a plan. We must be ready next time there is a knock. We do not know what to do, and then we do.

We practice, rehearse. Everyone has their role. Some start to think they are more important than others, but we make sure they know that everyone is equally important. There is a lot of head shaking. Crossing of arms. Finger pointing, that's a cliche, but we are doing it anyway. Hand waving, arguing without noise. The knock comes, like they knew when to strike. There is quiet panic. Some run away from the door, back into rooms. Some freeze. Some go to the floor like shooting will start. Two look at each other. Raise eyebrows and nod. They creep to the door. Get close and listen. One nods to the other. The other pauses. Thinks. Then leans into the door. They look at each other and nod again. Eyes closed and listening, the listening stretches.

the book cellar

Sometimes the hum makes him think of it. In the back of the store, above the Art & Photography section, the light hums. Coming from the stockroom he always hears it but usually can push by and put it out of mind. But today he stops and looks up, squinting with his mouth slack. Strains to listen. It's definitely humming, he says out loud. He thinks of the flat milky light it gives off, coming down and settling into his skin and starts scratching at his arms. Out of the corner of his eye he sees a customer watching him. Clears her throat. A question, he thinks, but he doesn't turn to her because the skin on his arms is starting to tingle and the sensation is moving up into his shoulders and across his chest. He struggles to keep his breathing even, convinced the light is burning into his skin like acid. He gives three strangled coughs and the customer moves away but he doesn't notice.

Richard?

He wonders how the customer knows his name, but it can't be a customer, he knows that voice. The itching is getting better, his breathing back to normal.

Richard? Are you okay?

He knows that voice, it's making him feel better, he feels calm and light. He turns toward the voice but sees only the milky light and thinks it might have gotten to her too, he can barely see her through it. Oh, hello Bertie.

Hello Richard. Are you okay?

He nods. Oh sure.

Because you've been standing here for 10 minutes looking at the ceiling.

Oh?

Yes you have.

Oh. Yes. Well. You see, it hums? It's humming.

She looks to the ceiling and says What? The light?

Yes. The light. He points to it.

She listens and shrugs and slowly nods. You're right it's humming.

Richard smiles and blinks and slowly the milky film fades from Bertie. Do these lights ever worry you?

What, the humming?

Not exactly, no. Well. No. Nothing, it's nothing.

You sure?

Sure. Quite.

Okay Richard. Listen, could you start on that Stieg Larsson display? It's almost break time.

Right. Of course. At the front of the centre island, correct?

Right.

Consider it done, he says and gives a quick salute. He watches Bertie walk away. She's wearing her navy blue pantsuit and Richard thinks *Today is Tuesday and on Tuesday Bertie normally wears her red dress.* He tries not to notice these things but they come to him anyway. He likes her in the red dress but the navy pantsuit is very nice even if it is

Tuesday. He opens his mouth to tell her, it would be alright to tell her, he should be able to, even if it isn't the red dress on Tuesday.

Bertie?

She stops and pauses with her navy blue back to him.

Bertie, I should clarify. I meant the fluorescent lights. I recall reading somewhere that they cause cancer. We work all day beneath them. Doesn't that worry you?

She turns, looks at him for a moment. She can almost see him shaking. *He always looks like a jackrabbit in hunting season,* Karl the part-timer once said. I hadn't thought about it, Richard.

But they cause cancer.

Where did you read this?

Well. I can't remember.

Richard, these days everything causes cancer. She smiles. You can't believe everything you read.

Richard jerks visibly and blinks at her. Twice.

How can you say that?

Everything in print is not always 100% correct. It can be wrong, it's written by humans after all. It's not all gospel.

Gospel. Is she religious? Richard often wonders about religious people, he thinks they know something he doesn't and that bothers him. But you manage a bookstore, he says.

So?

How can you manage a bookstore and question the printed word? It's sacred, like gospel. He spits *gospel* like a curse word, to get a reaction. To show Bertie he knows exactly what is going on but she doesn't seem to notice.

You're kidding, right? There's fact and fiction and sometimes the fact contains most of the fiction. She smiles but he just stares at her.

Oh, never mind Richard. She shakes her head. Sometimes I wonder about you.

He freezes. She wonders about him? What? Where? He wants to ask but can't. Maybe if she were wearing her red dress on the day she always wears it. Did she get her days confused and forget it was Tuesday?

Bertie thinks she has upset Richard because he's looking straight through her. She smiles wider. Richard, if you're worried about the lights giving you cancer you shouldn't stare at them.

Pardon? He blinks and she thinks *That's the way an owl blinks.* Large and almost mechanical.

Well, it's like a non-smoker worrying about lung cancer but takes up smoking. Right? She starts laughing lightly. Richard tries to copy her, tries to imply things with his laughter; *Ha ha! I know what you mean. Ha ha ha. I'm glad we can share a joke like this like I'm sure we can share so much if you would just give it a chance, Bertie. Ha ha.* Richard knows he's laughing too much but can't stop. He knows Bertie is wondering about him again in a way he doesn't want her to wonder about him but he can't get himself to stop. His face is twisting with the effort, making it look like he's in pain, physical agony. Bertie takes a step back and Richard's eyes widen, frightened that she might leave him like this, without a chance to explain. He starts waving his hands at her and the laughter slows and eventually stops and his face relaxes until it is almost back to normal.

Richard? Maybe you should get started on that display now.

Oh? Sure, of course. Yes. Enough horsing around, I guess. I haven't had a laugh like that in a while. Have you?

Not like that, no, she says slowly.

I just got laughing and couldn't stop. Have you ever seen those shows with the bloopers from movies and people are trying to say their lines but they can't get them out without cracking up? And then everyone around them starts cracking up and they start laughing at the *idea* of not being able to get their lines out and no one can stop laughing and they have to do several takes? Have you seen those?

I think so.

Right, it was like that with me, just now. Take 17! Ha.

Okay. Richard –

He cut her off. I was just wondering what you thought about the lights. Nothing serious, I was just making conversation. Nothing serious, right?

Mmm hmm.

Yes. He nods to the floor. Well, to the display! he says with a flourish of his hands, like he thinks an actor in a comedy would say it, to show Bertie everything is okay. Normal. He almost says normal out loud but catches himself.

Bertie looks at her watch. Maybe you should take your coffee break first.

Oh? Yes? Certainly. Of course. Big smile and another quick salute and he steps around her. He's walking like he's forgotten how to do it properly but he can't help it because he knows Bertie is watching. Take 18! he yells and tries to make his walk look like the way Charlie Chaplin walked, as if the odd stiffness in his gait is on purpose. He can't help but wonder if she notices he's wearing his blue sweater that he always wears on Tuesday. Richard thinks blue and red go nicely together but today it's the navy pant suit even though it's Tuesday.

The customer that was trying to get Richard's attention earlier comes to Bertie. He's an odd duck, isn't he?

Richard? Bertie starts to nod but changes it into a shrug and says Oh, he's okay. He just reads too much. He's harmless, really.

The customer looks at the books all around her and smiles. Reads too much? Well, this is some therapy, isn't it?

Richard goes down the mall to the coffee shop and gets a black French Roast and a lemon poppy seed low fat muffin. $3.83. He always has correct change and tips 25 cents. The girls at the coffee shop know his order and start getting it ready when they see him coming. He always takes his coffee and muffin back to the stock room. If he sees Bertie on his way to the back of the store he'll say Off to the book cellar.

Bertie thought of the name. There are no windows and the cinder-block walls are cold and there's always a breeze coming through the ill-fitted delivery door that leads to a road behind the mall that smells of gasoline and urine and rotting food. But Richard likes it because it is filled with books; shelves and stacks of them. And there are no fluorescent lights, just three bare bulbs on wires with pull chains, but the chains don't work the lights, there's a switch by the door. He turns the lights on and immediately feels better. He sees shadows slide about the room and move into the corners. There are no shadows with fluorescent lights, the milky light won't allow them, it covers them up. It's not natural.

He sits at the table and pulls his feet up under him and begins to read beneath the books that always seem ready to fall on him and if they did that would be just fine.

Richard thinks he hears Bertie call his name. Then she calls it again, then once more before he fully realizes it. Yes? Bertie?

I think that's long enough for your break.

He looks at the table, at his muffin with only the top eaten and then at the coffee, cold and untouched. He squeezes the book in his hand.

Richard?

Right. Yes. So sorry. I was wrapped up in this book, and time... well. I'm sorry. Quite.

It's okay, but you have to watch out for that. It's been happening quite a bit lately.

Yes. Understood. It won't happen again.

That's alright. Back to work?

Of course. Back to work.

For the rest of the morning Richard works quietly without looking at Bertie and when she reminds him about his lunch break he shakes his head and says he's not hungry and works through. When they close up she compliments him on the display and Richard nods and smiles. Bertie says he can take some paperbacks home. Bertie tears the covers off, winks and says Don't tell anyone.

A small smile. No, no. Of course not, Bertie. Mum's the word. She returns his smile, and Richard's cheeks flush at his shared secret with Bertie.

On the bus Richard notices he has a headache and he leans his forehead on the window, the glass cool. He watches people on the sidewalk, barely making their forms out in the dark. Like the shadows in the book cellar. He thinks of Bertie and the books she gave him. He quickly opens his bag and pulls them out. Two Timothy Findley's. A James Joyce reader, heavy and orange. He holds it up to his nose and breaths in, the smell light and heavy at the same time, wood chips. The smell of books always reminds him of his mother, but he can't remember why, she wasn't a reader. He puts the Joyce in the bag and looks at the other books. John le Carré. Three Robert B. Parker's. He sees his street, puts the rest of the books in the bag and pulls the bell. He lives in the top flat of a two storey house, his landlady in the bottom flat. At her door he knocks and she answers with a flashlight shining in his face. She always has the flashlight, no matter what time of day it is.

Oh, Richard. How nice, please come in.

I'm just on my way upstairs, Mrs Kaylin. For supper. Just wanted to drop these off, and he pulls out the three Robert B. Parker books.

Mrs Kaylin takes them and looks at the spines and says Oh, *Spenser*. My favourite.

I know.

Oh, thank you Richard.

You're welcome. Enjoy. But I must be going. I'm famished.

In his flat he goes to the cupboard beside the kitchen sink and takes out the aspirin bottle. He takes two without water, pauses, and takes another one. He looks out the window above the sink into the bedroom of the woman across the alley. She is sitting on her bed drinking a glass of wine. She gathers her hair absently in her free hand and lets it fall over the back of her white bathrobe. She does it again. There is only the bedside lamp on, and the shadow of her hair and arm float up and down the wall in the warm, low light. Richard closes the curtain and goes to another cupboard for a can of tomato soup. His secret is to add half a can of milk and half a can of water. Top it off with plenty of freshly ground pepper. Bertie would like that.

A knock while doing the dishes, Richard opens the door and sees Mrs Kaylin with a covered plate.

Hello, Richard. I brought you something to thank you for the books.

I was just about to start some coffee. Won't you come in?

Oh yes, thank you. Delighted, she says and enters unwrapping the plate to reveal Rice Krispie squares.

Oh my, I do like those. Richard turns to the percolator and starts the coffee.

Good. I hoped so. Yes. She seems quite pleased and sits down heavily at the kitchen table. She nods at the percolator. I haven't seen one of those in years.

I had to special order it. They still make them, but most stores don't carry them anymore. I just find the coffee tastes better.

Mrs Kaylin makes a small noise in her throat and smiles and looks at the squares at front of her. She thinks of having one, but decides to wait until the coffee is ready and Richard can join her. For minutes the room is silent except for the sound of the coffee brewing.

Have you read them?

Yes? Pardon me? She seems startled to find Richard in the same room with her.

I was wondering if you had already read the books I gave you.

Oh, no no. I haven't, no. Thank you again.

Good, fine. I'm pleased.

Silent again, percolator dancing.

Then Richard pours and creams and sugars for Mrs Kaylin. A Rice Krispie square each. Light sips from Richard, strong gulps from Mrs Kaylin.

Delicious.

Thank you.

Mrs Kaylin pauses and puts her cup down. She touches each fingertip to her knee and opens her mouth only to close it. Richard clears his throat and says Another cup, Mrs Kaylin?

Thank you, no. I'd never get to sleep. They both smile.

Another pause and she looks around the tidy kitchen and into the living room at the spilling bookcases and the stacks of books reaching halfway up the walls. She looks at her hands and sighs then raises her eyes to the ceiling. Finally she says Richard, what happened to the covers from the books?

He pulls back, smiles and nods and leans on his elbows, hunching into her. Well, you see Mrs Kaylin, at the bookstore there are some books that we have excess stock of, or they have been damaged or what have you. It's only with paperbacks, pocket books. We tear the covers off and send them to the distributor. They list the book as unsold and destroyed. Richard leans in further. But instead of destroying the books we give them to the employees.

We?

Yes. The manager. And... well... myself.

Are you the assistant manager?

Richard stares at his cup and picks it up but puts it down again. No. Not in title, no. But my duties are quite extensive.

Really?

Yes. Generally, I'm in charge of displays. Large displays throughout the store. It's quite a large store.

Is it?

Fairly large, yes. I've gotten quite the compliment on my displays. A good display can positively impact the sales of a book. I think it's my responsibility to do my best on a display. After all, a writer can spend years crafting his art. I owe it to him, or her, to make sure I do everything in my power to ensure the public sees it, and sees it in the best possible way.

Yes. People should take pride in their work.

Absolutely. It's always been my feeling that a man in my position *must* take pride in his work. Lead by example, as they say.

Mrs Kaylin nods and says Quite the example.

Over the next half hour Richard tells more stories from the store, describes his displays, tells her what remaindered books are. They mark them with a marker? she says with her eyebrows raised and Richard solemnly nods. He only feels slightly guilty for stretching the truth. But is it really that much of a stretch? He does do quite a lot at the store. And where would Bertie be without his displays? Bertie. Wednesday tomorrow and Bertie wears her grey sweater Wednesdays unless the navy pant suit threw everything off. He will wear his black sweater tomorrow, just in case. Black goes with almost everything. That would be the smart thing to do. Expect the unexpected, he read that somewhere. Where? Bertie would like that one. Where did he read it? He'll try to work it into conversation tomorrow, maybe if Bertie takes her break at the same time he does. How many people are on tomorrow? He wants to get the schedule from his desk but stops himself. Maybe he'll even buy Bertie her coffee, the girls at the coffee shop would have a field day with that one, an extra coffee and muffin *What's up?* they'd say and he'd wink and tap his nose in an *entre nous* fashion and they'd ooh and ahh and he'd leave them smiling and wondering. Walk into the store with two coffees and two muffins, say Expect the unexpected. No, that doesn't make sense. Maybe sitting at the table in the book cellar with her he can say it, make it sound natural, and she'll lean in and laugh and he'll do the same and quite forgetting where he is and who he's with, Richard reaches out and touches Mrs Kaylin's hand. He looks down and says Oh.

Well, Richard, it's been lovely but I must be going.

Richard pulls his hand back and says Of course. Well. Thank you for the squares.

Certainly.

Yes. I have an early day tomorrow. My mind is elsewhere. On my work, elsewhere. I have this headache and I'm not quite thinking straight. You know how it is with headaches. You understand. The lights at work bother me.

Mrs Kaylin pushes herself up and Richard leaps to pull back her chair. He moves to the door, opens it and says Goodnight. She avoids his eyes and says Thank you, goodnight.

He watches her go down the stairs, slightly sideways, with her skirt raised in one hand revealing her thick ankles, the straps of her shoes bulging the flesh. The skin a dark red, almost purple like a plum. He closes the door softly and moves to the kitchen sink and puts cold water on his face. His headache is worse, concentrated on the right side of his head and into his ear and down the neck and shoulder. He dries his hands and pushes the curtain aside but the window across the alley is dark. He turns and leans against the sink and looks at the cups and plates on the table and tells himself to never, ever forget where he is and who he's with. Never.

In the morning his headache is worse, the pain now into his right eye and all across his back and when he lifts himself out of bed he buckles under a wave of nausea. He goes to the bathroom and kneels in front of the toilet and opens his mouth. He starts to drool a bit, but nothing else. He can't bring himself to stick a finger down his throat, that seems unclean, so he waits until the nausea lessens. When it does he gets up and notices a pain in his abdomen. He touches a spot on his right side under his ribs and winces. He goes to the sink and washes and avoids the mirror and dresses, almost forgetting the black sweater. Doesn't eat and leaves for work, walking slowly to the bus stop in a bright sun and watches his shadow in front of him. He thinks of the fluorescent lights at work and the pain gets worse.

The mall is quiet, empty, the stores still gated and shadowed. He stops in front of the bookstore and before rattling the gate to be let in he takes a deep breath and wipes his hands across his sticky forehead. He coughs and shakes the gate and gives a cheery Hello?

Karl the part-timer lets him in. Karl is young, university young, long hair and those black and white hi-top sneakers like they wore in the '50s. How goes it, Richard?

It goes well, thank you. Yourself?

Oh, you know. Here I am, getting my minimum wage.

Yes. Well. Alright, another day, here we go. Wednesdays are usually slow, he says.

After lunch he is feeling a bit better, stocking the Sports & Recreation section. He steps to pick up a stack of books when he hears a crunch, feels something beneath his shoe. He looks down and reaches and picks up a pewter chain and pendant. The pendant is a flat rounded cross with four pictures of Jesus at each point on the front, on the back some writing. *I am a Catholic. Please call a priest.* He rubs the cross with a fingertip and pools the chain in his palm and wonders what religion he is. It may be Catholic, there's no reason why it couldn't be Catholic. How nice it must be, to have a priest come when you need them, all because of writing on a necklace. He would know what to do, place a hand on a forehead, *Be calm my child, all is forgiven in the eyes of God.*

How nice that must be, to be able to tell people these things, and for them to believe you because you are a priest and they are a Catholic.

Richard looks around and sees no customers and walks into the book cellar. He loosens his tie and tries to put the chain around his neck but the clasp is broken. He finds a roll of tape and fixes the chain as best as he can and slips it over his head and feels the cool weight of it against his chest.

Bertie couldn't go to break at the same time so Richard sulkily only buys one coffee and muffin. Expect the unexpected, he says to the coffee girl but she doesn't know what he's talking about. Karl is in the book cellar when he gets back, reading the paper. He starts talking about one of the articles. Richard tries to read and ignore him but eventually puts down his book.

Police don't have any leads. The fires seem to be set at random, no pattern. Nothing. Just a fucking nutcase if you ask me.

Richard nods. Yes. Well. Perhaps. He probably has his reasons.

Karl looks over his paper at him. Right. His reason is because he's a nutcase. That's his reason.

Richard looks around him at the books. If you tapped the lightbulbs and let them swing on their wires the shadows they caused made it look like the shelves of books around the stockroom were on fire. Richard almost stands up to make the bulbs swing but doesn't. Maybe he likes the sound, he says.

The sound?

Yes. Have you ever listened closely to a fire? Karl shrugs. Quite mesmerizing it is, Karl. All those snaps and crackles. Whomever lit that fire created those sounds, controls them. Like a composer. Or a symphony conductor.

Right.

Yes, like a conductor, Richard says and goes back to his book.

Bertie opens the door. Karl? When you're done break, could you bring the box of Berlitz books?

What do you think, Bertie?

She steps inside. About what?

Richard here thinks that an arsonist is like a conductor. Symphony conductor, not a train one. How about you?

What? I don't know. She looks at Richard, smiling at her. I guess, she says. She cranes out the door and looks for any stray customers, then ducks back in. I suppose there's an inherent power to fires, and the person lighting them probably feels they are in control of that power. I guess...

Richard nods rapidly and looks at Karl and says I'm glad you agree, Bertie. I knew you would understand. He looks at her, her hair is different. Short, it's always short, but it's styled differently. She's never changed her hairstyle, not in the 3 years he has known her. Same hair, always red nail polish and red lipstick. Bright glossy red that sometimes got on her teeth and Richard would think of slowly pushing his finger past her lips, into her mouth, and wiping the red from her teeth.

Karl startles Richard by standing up and shaking his head. Bertie gives him a small shrug and a smile and he picks up the box and leaves. Richard watches Bertie to see if she is still thinking about the fires.

Richard, you don't look well.

All of a sudden, Richard feels his headache again, and the burning spot in his stomach restarts. Well, now that you mention it, I haven't felt well the past couple of days. Headache, pain in my stomach. He points to the spot just under his ribs and when he does the pain gets worse and a gurgling sound comes from his throat.

Are you okay?

I'll be fine. He smiles broadly. He sees the way Bertie is looking at him and he knows that she thinks he is weak because he can't handle a little pain. I'm quite alright, he says and rolls his shoulders like the cowboys in movies and when he does he feels a sharp stab in his stomach and he grimaces.

Maybe you should go home.

No, I'm fine really. Don't worry.

No, I insist. I need you back here tomorrow well rested and healthy, right? You're important to this store. She puts her hand on his shoulder and Richard looks at it and the grey sweater just above it and at how well it goes with his black sweater. Then he nods.

On the bus the pain gets worse and he starts to perspire, the sweat rolling into his eyes. He wipes it away and looks out the window and sees everything double and closes his eyes tightly. He feels like he's floating and his right ear is ringing and the pain through his body is making him nauseous again. He thinks he's going to vomit and opens his eyes and stands up and yells at the bus driver, the driver shakes his head and starts on about regulations and that he can only stop at designated stops and Richard starts screaming and the passengers turn to look at him and the driver stares at him in the mirror and then pulls over.

Richard stumbles from the bus and leans over, lets his mouth hang open but nothing comes. He straightens and looks to see where he is and realizes he has missed his stop by a block. He walks back to his flat and gets the door open and finds his way to bed. The pain seems deeper, rooted in his bones now and he tries to get up for some aspirin but can't lift his body. He closes his eyes and hopes for sleep but it doesn't come. His whole body is hot and he squirms on the bed, his skin wet and thick and rubbery like an eel. He opens his eyes and sees the sun through the window and the bright of it hurts so he closes them again. When he next opens them the window is dark and the room is still and he stares at the ceiling and whimpers when he sees the flames and in the middle of it all, Bertie. *I love fires don't you Richard isn't the sound incredible Richard isn't the power of it all incredible Richard what can it be like to contain that much power Richard RichardRichardRichard* and just when Bertie leans in to kiss him, her lips redder than any red he has ever seen, the perfect red, his eyes close, he tries not to let them but he can't help it, he says Bertie? But she is gone and he sinks, lets himself sink because she is gone and there is no reason not to sink, sink into something black and for a moment it seems like that is all there ever will be, black, but then he's on a boat, on black water and he is rowing and there is no land in sight.

In the morning his fever is down slightly but the pain is still there and his vision blurry. Richard seems confused to find the ceiling isn't burnt and there is no rowboat. His room is fine, his bed sheets are twisted and damp, but his room is normal. He slept in his clothes and they are also damp. He falls out of bed. I have to go to work, he says. I have to tell Bertie something. He vomits while fixing his tie, a thick grey pool on his bedroom floor. He wipes his mouth on his sweater sleeve and it leaves a slug's trail and he wipes at it with his hand. The ringing is in both ears, lower now, almost a hum and he thinks of the lights at work and their milky light all over him, sucking away his shadows.

The mall is already open, people stare at him. He walks unsteadily into the store, falls into his Stieg Larsson display, the books falling under and over him. Bertie! he yells, Bertie! and he hears running footsteps and things go dark.

Richard! Wake up! Bertie is holding a wet paper towel to his forehead. He looks up at her. She's wearing her red dress. Richard holds his sleeve up to hers. Red and black, that's fine. It sounds familiar. He thinks and remembers. It's a book title. He says *The Red and the Black* out loud and Bertie pauses and blinks at him and says Stendhal? and Richard smiles and says I knew you would understand.

My God, Richard, you blacked out.

God, yes. Wait. Richard reaches under the neck of his sweater, pulls his tie aside and digs into his shirt and fingers the cross still there and pulls it out. Call a priest, Bertie. I'm a Catholic. Did you know that Bertie?

No, Richard, listen, I'm taking you to the hospital.

No, call a priest, I have to tell him something. No, he says, I have to tell *you* something. He tries to remember what it is, why can't he remember? It's so important and he can't remember. He closes his eyes and sees his ceiling from last night and the moving shadows on the books in the book cellar and he remembers. It wouldn't be so bad to tell her, even if it wasn't true? Just to stretch the truth a bit wouldn't be so bad. Lie a little to her, but the lie being something to let her know that he has power in him, control of something large and beautiful and that he isn't weak. She said she loved fire, didn't she? He can fib, tell her he lit the fires, he conducts the symphony, wouldn't that be okay? A lie to benefit both of them? He clutches the cross and tries to look to the back of the store. Customers have circled. He cranes around them and sees the door. The book cellar. Book seller. Book cellar, bookseller. Oh I get it Bertie. It's a pun, I get it. They call her Bertie because Bertice is her full name and she hates it. He would never call her Bertice, and she would never call him Rick, they wouldn't do that to each other, a relationship has to be built upon respect. Bertie, come closer. I have to tell you something, he says. She moves close, so close his lips are on her ear and his nose buried in her hair. She smells of books. What is it Richard? He opens his mouth and closes his eyes and thinks of the books he's sprawled over, that they feel better than any bed and he pulls at the cross and the tape gives and it falls to the floor and he says Oh Bertie.

reasons why I can't sit in my favourite booth at Stillman's anymore

My mother makes her eyes and mouth into big circles because she isn't used to me ringing her doorbell and the big circles are meant to display shock and surprise but I'm not falling for it, I don't fall for it, because she has been doing the circle thing to me for forty (40) years, no probably more but I don't remember much from the years from zero to eight. Except that time I had to get hernia surgery when I was four (4) or five (5), before school age, I was born with it, and I remember crossing the street with my mother leaving the cab and going into the hospital and I remember waking up in the recovery room crying and the nurse not saying anything but winding up a Fisher Price toy and the music quieted me and even at four (4) or five (5) I had the slight feeling of shame that I had been crying, and I remember my uncle asking me in my hospital bed if I wanted anything and I said a red dinky car. A car that I kept for years until a neighbour kid named Randall stole it with all my other dinky cars and took a rock and smashed them all, even though he denied it. Jamie, a friend who lied constantly said Randall did it, he saw him do it, and although Jamie's word was more suspect than not, I believed him. Randall was a foster kid, so we all let it go. But here's my mother with her circle eyes and mouth, she makes them go bigger, I can see even through the screen door, when I ask if I can borrow dad. The big circles now seem real, where before when I first knocked they seemed there just for effect, to make me feel something that I don't really bother to feel anymore.

She lets me in, gives me green tea at the kitchen table, asks me if I'm taking my medication, no, asks me if I'm drinking still, yes. She nods and looks away, past me, into the living room. We are quiet and I try to drink the tea without making any noise, but when I swallow it seems horrendously loud, like a boulder being dropped into a lake, so I stop drinking the tea. I try to breathe as little as possible to keep the wind tunnel noise it seems to be creating from filling the room. But I can feel my heartbeat in my ears and it is getting faster and my hands and lips are tingling, going numb and my mother tells me to breathe in through my nose and out my mouth and I try but it's not working, the thing bursts at the base of my spine and starts its slow climb up my back and I know if it reaches my head I'll be gone for a while, away somewhere that takes a long time to come back from. I stand up quickly and start pacing the kitchen, breath coming hard and painful, I start rapidly tapping my right thumbnail against my bottom teeth, sometimes this calms me, I don't know why. It's not working. My mother stands up and grabs me and makes me stop. Tells me to close my eyes and fold my hands behind my head and to breathe. In the nose. Out the mouth. Slowly. Again. Slowly. Think of something good. Happy. Something good that makes me happy. I do. I'm not going to tell you what it is because you'll probably find it shallow and stupid, and also because if I say it out loud it might stop being something happy and good for me. My mother keeps saying Good and Again and eventually the thing stops its climb and I can't hear my heartbeat in my ears and I sit down and drink some tea, going cold but it doesn't matter and I ask her again if I can borrow dad.

The first time the thing crawled up my spine and made it to my head was outside my PhD advisor's office. I was waiting to go in, present what I had so far on ordinal analysis in proof theory. I've always had a thing for numbers. Counting things and putting them into categories based on characteristics and then taking those same numbers and putting them into different categories based on new characteristics. There is order and logic in numbers, yes, but there also room for art and beauty. A space created by numbers, that space waiting to be filled with more numbers, arranged and ordered, crossing and tumbling over each other, a constant chase, then being caught, then the chase again. Like Glenn Gould playing Bach. I don't know, I don't really like to think about it anymore, can't listen to Bach anymore. There's a part of me that still loves numbers, but a bigger part that blames those numbers for the way I am. People say I'm better than I was. Can carry a conversation now. I don't know. I still catch myself turning things into numbers. I had to stop sitting in the last booth at Stillman's, my favourite, because it is the sixth (6th) booth and six (6) is the first perfect number. Perfect numbers being a sum of all its positive divisors except itself. $1+2+3=6$. Perfect. That's the beauty I mentioned earlier. I had to stop sitting in that sixth (6th) perfect booth because the wall is covered in old photographs of the neighbourhood. Twenty-eight (28) of them. Twenty-eight (28) being the next perfect number. $1+2+4+7+14=28$. See where this is going? Twelve (12) are in square frames, sixteen (16) in rectangular. Twenty-two (22) are matted, Six (6) are not. They are all (28) black and white, all (28) in black frames. Except for their size and shape, all (28) the frames are identical in style. Twenty-seven (27) of the photographs have cars in them; nineteen (19) have one (1) car, three (3) have two (2) cars, five (5) have three (3) cars, and one (1), a long street shot taken in front of the bar sometime in the 1950s, has twenty-eight (28). It is the last photograph on the right, making it the twenty-eighth (28th). Twenty-eight (28) photographs on the wall, this being the twenty-eighth (28th) containing twenty-eight (28) cars. Needless to say, it's my favourite. There is more grouping and regrouping I have done with the photographs-people: male, female, hats no hats, looking at camera, not looking at camera, but I can't get into that right now. Rabbit hole or something. I don't know. I didn't stick with the therapy appointments very long. Anyway, apparently the PhD advisor came into the hall to find me on the floor. Don't get me wrong, this wasn't out of the blue, there were signs, early on, but it got worse in high school. Almost perfect marks, but little else to show that I was a human being. Only leaving the basement to go to school, forgetting to eat for a couple of days, rarely showering or changing my clothes. Long stretches of staring as my mind worked through problems, or the grouping and regrouping. Mostly non verbal except in class, and that speech barely recognizable as human, more like something an early computer created. No friends, obviously, and more obviously, no girlfriends. No interest from either side.

My mother slowly and softly places her fingertips on the kitchen table like a pianist preparing to begin a piece. Just as slowly and softly she asks why I want to borrow dad. I tell her. She listens and does her best not to make her eyes circle wide and something about that effort gets to me. I get a hitch in my speech, and I make one of those deep-breath-I'm-not-going-to-cry noises and she nods through the rest of my speech and says Yes, I can borrow dad.

When I was eight (8), my mother saw me watching a baseball game on television. I had been watching the game, but at the point she saw me I was deep in a stare, organizing all the numbers the announcers were saying. At bats. Batting average. Walks. Strikeouts. Hits. Runs. Singles. Doubles Triples. Home runs. Two (2) run home runs. Three (3) run home runs. Grand Slams (4). Runs batted in. Something tilted. Later, my mother asked me about baseball. I asked her if she could could get me a book. A book with all the baseball numbers. That's the way I phrased it, baseball numbers. She nodded her head vigorously, as if the speed of her nods could encourage my normalcy. She came home the next day after her last class was taught with a pocket book, *The Complete All*Time Pro Baseball Register.* I found out baseball numbers were called statistics, stats. It had the stats of every player up to 1975. I opened it up at a random page and looked at the headers: TEAM BY YEAR. BIRTH DATE. HGT. WGT. G. AB. R. H. 2B. 3B. HR. RBI. BB. SO. SB. BA. SA. I went to another page, the pitcher's section. W. L. PCT. SV. G. GS. CG. IP. H. BB. SO. ShO. ERA. AB. H. HR. BA. And row upon row of numbers. I did an odd thing and smiled, and I felt my mother go still, not wanting to do something to break what in most other houses would just be a pleasant but standard moment, while here it was the moon landing. She watched me as I closed the book and looked at the cover. A picture of grass with a white ball. The ball had red marks, stitches, that I resisted counting, knowing that the number wouldn't be correct, as there were stitches I couldn't see. Above that I read

Every player in major league baseball, 1901-1975
Complete career records!
Thirteen categories for batters!
Seventeen categories for pitchers!
Plus single season leaders, league by league, for batters
and pitchers, and All-Time leaders!

Remember the rabbit hole I mentioned earlier? This was my first rabbit hole. Actually, I spent most of my time in rabbit holes, that was my reality. It was when I wasn't in one that things weren't right, like my mother watching me smile at a baseball book. That was my odd. I wish it wasn't that way. But it was.

I looked up from the book at my mother and noticed she was holding a vinyl bag like some of the kids I went to school with used as a book bag. Adidas. A stick poking out of it. She pulled the stick out and it wasn't a stick but a baseball bat. Then she pulled out a glove and a few (3) balls. Then a hat that she tried to put on my head but I ducked away. We both paused and something made me put my hand out for the hat and I put it on. She smiled and I didn't count her teeth that were visible.

Mom goes to get dad and I go into the pantry and open the door to the garage. The smell of lawnmower gas and tires. I peer until my eyes adjust and I see the bag and go to it. Open and see the glove and baseballs. The bat, where is the bat. Look and it's leaning against the wall with some rakes and shovels. I don't need to find the hat because I'm wearing it. I have been wearing it for almost forty (40) years, almost everywhere. The colours are faded, the red and blue a light memory of what they were, the white now a milk tea grey. The elastic at the back is totally broken down, and the hat just sits on my head now, ready to be kidnapped by any small mention of wind.

I go back into the house, into the kitchen, and mom is standing there with dad. I go to the cupboard under the sink and reach out a plastic grocery bag, take the urn from mom and put it in the plastic bag, double knotting the handles, and placing it gently into the vinyl Adidas bag, zipper it and nod. Mom nods and touches my shoulder and I don't flinch. I stay under her hand and she leaves it there for a bit, too long, really, but I don't say anything because I rarely let it happen and she did let me borrow dad after all and we all have to give something to get along in this world. Someone told me that. It might have been one of the therapists I stopped going to, I don't know. Maybe Mary at Stillman's. It doesn't matter.

What was said to convince my mother that letting me take dad in a vinyl Adidas bag was a fine and reasonable act: I saw a news story last year during the World Series of how a longtime Chicago Cubs fan promised his father they would listen to the Cubs win the series together, whenever that happened. The news report showed the son in a lawn chair with a portable radio and a light shining on his father's gravestone. I remember watching the report sitting at the bar in Stillman's. Most everyone around me got teary eyed and quiet and when I said the dad has no idea if the Cubs win or not because he's dead the line of drinkers (6) spun to me and began grumbling and muttering, all of which amounted to That's not the point. But when I asked what was the point, I just got sad looks and headshakes. I get a lot of sad looks and headshakes, I know what they mean. So I need to find the point of seeing your favourite team win a major championship with your dead father. That might be a key for me, unlocking what makes me get all those sad looks and headshakes. I want to be one of the people giving them, not receiving them.

Something you shouldn't do while on the Number 1 bus going from your mother's house to downtown: take an urn from your Adidas bag and unscrew the lid to see what the ashes of your dead father look like.

My uncle taught me how to throw different pitches. Two (2) seam fastball. Four (4) seam fastball. Curve. Change up. The change up being my favourite. You make an okay sign with your hand and nestle the ball deep in your palm. When you look at the ball in your hand it looks like your thumb and forefinger are touching to make a zero (0). As a pitcher, that's what you want the opposing team to do against you. Zero (0) hits, zero (0) walks, zero (0) runs. Perfect. The day my uncle taught me those pitches he found me at the field behind my school. I was twelve (12). I would go there with my bag of equipment and take the bat and three (3) balls I had and toss them up to myself and hit them into the outfield, go and gather them and repeat. I saw my uncle watching in his work clothes that were a colour somewhere between green and brown. His workboots with the leather wearing thin at the steel toes. He would often come to my house after work to see if my mother needed anything done. Lawnmowing. Storm windows. He had wavy hair, slicked back, and a moustache that looked like a drawing. If you traded his work clothes for a suit he would look like someone from a black and white movie, someone who gets the girl at the end but doesn't really care if he does or not. He came out onto the field and reached into my bag and pulled out my glove and passed it to me. He took the bat and leaned it against the backstop.

He took the three (3) balls and walked out to the pitching rubber and motioned me behind home plate, pointing down to get me into a catcher's crouch. Then he gripped a baseball, held his hand out and rotated it to show me the grip and then said what the grip was. He did this for four (4) pitches. The four (4) seam fastball came at me straight. The two (2) seam jerked down hard at the end, moving away from the centre of the plate. The curve floated high and then fell perfectly across the plate. The change up looked like the four (4) seam until it dropped suddenly and I had to turn my glove over to catch it before it hit the ground. He said Your arm angle should always be the same. He said Same with your armspeed. Every pitch should look like it's going to be your four (4) seam. He said Disrupting the batter's timing is key. Then he said Okay? And I nodded and he nodded and left. Soon after the equipment went to live in the garage and I went to the basement, we talked about that already.

There are one hundred and eight (108) stitches in a baseball. One hundred and eight (108) is not a perfect number.

I get off the bus and go a street below Barrington, towards the waterfront. I go into a building with a blue and gold plaque by the door that says the building is very old, and because it is so very old some society thinks it's worthy of this plaque. There is a number on the plaque. 1751. So very old. I go down the stairs into the basement and don't go to the sixth (6th) booth, don't look at the twenty-eight (28) photographs there, don't think about perfect numbers, sit at the bar not thinking about what number stool it is, not looking at the bottles lined at the mirror behind the bar so I don't count them, take the urn out of its bags and put it on the bartop. Sean looks at the urn and then me and gets a coaster and picks up the urn and drops the coaster and sets the urn on top. Pauses, then breaks into hacking laughter. The few (4) at the bar join him. This is what passes for jokes here.

What time is the baseball game on?

Sean shrugs and gets the remote and presses buttons and a guide comes on the screen. Presses some more buttons and a blue bar high-lights the game. 9 (nine) pm.

What time is it now?

Sean gestures at the screen with the remote, the time is in the top right hand corner of the guide. 4:03 (four zero three) pm. I order a draught, I want to take things slow.

I only met my father once (1). I was thirty-nine (39) at the time. I looked him up online and went to find him. He was in another province, taught at a university like my mother. When I knocked and he opened the door he stared then nodded and asked me in. I didn't talk much. He said he wanted to marry my mother, but she didn't want that, she didn't want to be married at nineteen (19). He said he sent her money for a while but she wrote him after a time and said she didn't need his money anymore. He said a lot about my mother not wanting things. I wasn't interested. I stopped listening. I watched him to see if he noticed the baseball hat on my head, to see if he would see the hat and ask Is that your favourite team? He didn't. He didn't ask me anything, too busy telling me what my mother didn't want.

The therapist I went to for a very short time asked me about that, asked if I was resentful of having a father that wasn't present, didn't make a large attempt to make his presence felt, whether that effected the way I presented myself to the world, effected the way I saw the world. I said I didn't know. She kept asking the same questions in slightly different ways, I kept saying I didn't know. I wasn't very good at therapy.

When I got home my mother asked how it went. I said fine, he seems nice enough, I don't really look like him. My mother nodded, eyes going wide then going back to normal when I didn't say things she was expecting me to say. I don't know what those things were, but I knew I didn't say them.

At my third (3rd) draught, the woman beside me, Mary, asks who is in the urn.

My father.

Oh, I'm sorry.

It's okay. I didn't really know him.

Shit, that's shitty. I'm sorry.

It's fine, really.

Do you want to talk about it?

Not really.

I think you should talk about it. It will make you feel better. People always feel better getting things off their chest. Like criminals? They always say it's like a weight lifted when they finally confess.

I'm not a criminal.

That's not what I'm saying. I just think you'll feel better if you let it out.

I stare at her for a bit, nodding. Thanks, but I just want to watch the baseball game.

She looks at the tv on the wall, on it there are five (5) women sitting around a table laughing. What baseball game? She says.

It's coming.

She watches me. I try not to look at her from the corner of my eye, but I do. I see her look at my almost empty glass, looks at Sean, points to my glass, points to herself, and Sean pulls and pours and sets the glass in front of me and I nod. Look at her and nod again.

She says You don't have to be like this. You know, people are generally kind, they want to help when someone needs help. You come in here everyday. Drink all night.

So do you.

I know, she says.

Are you waiting for a kindness from someone? I say it in a way I don't mean to say. I can see it bite her, see her eyes flicker at the pain. But I don't apologise. Things would be worse then.

She nods and smiles and turns to her drink and says Enjoy the game.

How my mother ended up with an urn full of my father's ashes that I only met once, didn't even see him at his funeral: he just showed up in a box with a courier because a lawyer said that's what my father wanted.

I don't take things slow after that. I start ordering shots with my draught. I keep asking the time, getting louder each time. It is nowhere near 9 (nine) o'clock. It is getting hard to stay in my stool, like someone is pushing it. I get up and try to walk a straight line to the bathroom, manage to piss without getting any on me. Try to ignore the thing wanting to burst in my spine. Go to the sink and splash water on my face. Slap at my cheeks to try and stop the slow listing in my head. Avoid my eyes in the mirror. Hard breaths into my nose and out my mouth. Drink some water from the tap. More hard breaths. Think about putting a finger down my throat but don't.

More water. More slaps. Dry off and go back to my stool. Sit for a second then stand and gather the urn and drop it into the bag. Leave the bar and up the stairs into the cool fall air. That's better. I slowly walk around the back of the so very old building. Into the alley with a dumpster and its stink. I pull the urn out and put it in front of the wall. My feet are size 9 (nine). In shoes they are twelve (12) inches long. I walk toe to heel from the urn. Sixty (60) feet, six (6) inches. The distance from home plate to the pitching rubber. I put my bag down and pull out my glove and three (3) baseballs. Put one (1) ball in my hand and the other two (2) by the bag. Get set up and stare at the urn. Nod and get a four (4) seam fastball grip, wind up and throw. I watch it go high over the urn, thudding off the brick wall. I get another ball, the urn gives me the sign for the two (2) seam. This one (1) sinks hard at the urn, bounces beside it, then skips off the wall. I pick up the last ball. Stare in. Change up. I get my grip, then look at it, look at the perfect zero (0) my thumb and index finger make, almost get lost in the beauty of it, like a vortex, but I don't. There is a game to finish, one last batter to get. I wind up and let the ball go.

Stephen Hines lives in Dartmouth, Nova Scotia, Canada with his wife and son. *the late season* is his first book of short stories.

September 2017

This first edition is published as a
trade paperback; there are 126 numbered
& lettered copies signed by the author, & handbound
in boards by the Tangerine Press, Tooting, London;
numbered copies contain a print by photographer
Jeff Brouws; lettered copies contain original
artwork by Stephen Hines.